MY GIFT

....

Jules May

Contents

0

He was lying on a bed of orchids, unconscious. The white petals tickled his small, upturned nose, while his curly hair jutted out in stark contrast to the neatly groomed plants. The light from the morning sun casted a spotty, jagged pattern of shadows across his high cheekbones. His lips, cracked and pale, had a tiny trickle of blood escaping down his porcelain skin.

Jade squatted down and, using a tree branch she stole from her tomato tree, poked at his face from a distance.

For a while, he didn't move. Ah, is he dead?

Then, he stirred.

Nope, nope, alive! This Earthling is still alive! Jade instinctively moved backwards and fell on her butt.

She was about to cry for help when his long eyelashes fluttered open. Large, brown irises stared right into Jade —so dazed yet so dazzling at the same time. Instantly, the scream disappeared from her throat and was replaced by a small gasp. The first thought that came to her mind was: wow, he's... gorgeous.

The next thought: okay, no, get it together, Jade, he's still an Earthling.

"H- Hello," she muttered.

The man blinked a few times before pushing himself off the ground. "Where... Where am I?" he croaked.

"Paradys."

"Where?" He looked around, slowly taking in the scenery of Jade's garden. "Am I still in Chicago?"

"Is that a place on Earth?" Jade couldn't help but chuckle. "No, silly, you are in a totally different realm. The realm of Paradys."

"Realm? What?" The man still did not seem to comprehend what she was saying. His curious eyes darted around the flowering vines lining the ceiling and the rows of potted plants. "Is this a farm or something? Am I in a different country?"

Jade smiled in response. Waking up to an Earthling inside her garden was not what she expected her Monday morning to start off with, but this man did not even know about the existence of other realms. He must just be a regular, peasant Earthling, not those scary ones with Gifts. She breathed a small sigh of relief; there was nothing to be afraid of, it seemed.

"You're in my garden," she explained. "My name is Jade. What's yours?"

"Ryan." His voice was low and silky, like barrel-aged honey. "How... did I get here?"

Jade peered at Ryan. He seemed genuinely confused about his situation. "I don't know either. This is quite a distance away from Earth. Do you remember what happened before this?"

Ryan frowned. "I... I really don't know... I was looking for food, and then I fell asleep, and then... somehow I'm here." As if on command, his stomach rumbled through his crumpled T-shirt. He covered it sheepishly. "I'm still really hungry."

"Do they not have food where you live?"

"They do, I just- I just don't have money to buy it."

Jade had to stop herself from laughing at that. Wasn't Earth supposed to be the realm for 'peace and prosperity'? Then why couldn't their people afford to eat? The First Lady was indeed a 'load of bullshit', as her father always said.

"I'll get you some food, but you must promise to stay here and remain hidden," she warned. "People here don't like anybody from Earth."

"Oh, why is that?"

Jade stared at the Earthling incredulously. "You really don't know anything, do you?" she probed. "Your First Lady has been trying to force our realm to submit to her rule for years now."

"First Lady Elena?" Ryan appeared to be even more perplexed by Jade's answer. "Why would she do that?"

Well, no matter how clueless he was, at least he still knew who the First Lady was. He probably had to —she was Earth's ruler, after all. "She's been doing that to all the realms. Any realm that refused to submit will be threatened with those monsters with Gifts," Jade said bitterly. "But our realm has been doing well resisting them so far, though. Our battlers are very strong, and they have been stopping those terrifying monsters from coming into our realm. But..." Her voice cracked. "It's still terrible. It's never-ending war. My grandfather died in one of the battles a while ago."

Ryan's expression softened. "Oh... I'm- I'm so sorry, Jade," he mumbled. His coffee brown eyes were shimmering in the light, as if they were filled with tears.

Jade sighed. "You don't have to be, it's not your fault anyway." She managed a reassuring smile. "You're just a regular person."

Ryan's sympathetic eyes were still boring into Jade, which was making her blush a little. She quickly stood up to change the subject. "Stay here, I'll- I'll get some food for you."

She sprinted out of the garden and back along the familiar, winding path up the hill. A homey cottage perched on the hill, overlooking the rest of the quaint, modest town. Inside, her mother had just finished clearing up the dishes, and was wiping the kitchen counter. Seeing a flustered Jade rushing into the house, she raised her head and wiped her olive-skinned hands on the apron.

"Hey, Jadey bird, what's wrong? You're back early."

Jade wasted no time in getting straight to the point. "Do we have any leftovers from breakfast?"

Her mother grinned. "What, is there a cat crashing at your garden again?"

"S- Something like that..." Jade mumbled uneasily. As much as she hated keeping secrets, she couldn't let anybody find out about

Ryan. If they did, the entire Paradys military would show up at their front door. They wouldn't even care that Ryan was a normal civilian without a Gift; to the adults, all Earthlings were 'monsters of terror' or 'omens of death'. They'd kill him immediately. Also, her precious garden would probably be demolished too, and she can't let that happen.

"Check the bottom of the fridge." Her mother gestured with her head before returning to her chores. "Oh, and don't forget to come back in time for lunch! Your father is coming back from his duty station today."

"Okay, thanks, Mom!" she chirped before scampering out of the house again.

For the next few days, Jade sneaked food to Ryan regularly. Her family was very used to her spending all her time in her little oasis of nature, and she definitely made use of that to hang out more with the mysterious Earthling man. In exchange, Ryan had been helping her tend to her plants. He was surprisingly meticulous and thoughtful, and her plants bloomed to twice their original sizes after only a few days.

With replenished energy, Ryan was also looking... even more gorgeous, if possible. His brown eyes were now sparkling with energy, and his lips were now pink and full. Every time he saw her, he would drop whatever he was doing and greet her in the most excited, puppy-like manner. And every time he did that, Jade's heart would skip a beat.

Today, Jade was greeted with a handmade flower crown.

She had devoured her lunch as fast as she could to go back to the garden. And there Ryan was, waiting inside as usual, but this time with a present.

"I'm finally done," Ryan said cheerfully, holding out the wreath of flowers. "This is for you."

Jade gaped at the crown; it was a combination of all the flowers in her garden —orchids, tulips, daisies, peonies— painstakingly crafted into a perfect ring. "Oh, Ryan... You didn't have to..."

"No, I had to," Ryan insisted. "You're the kindest person I've ever met, Jade, and I want you to have this." With that, he tenderly placed the flower crown on top of Jade's head.

Jade could not help but giggle airily. This was the sweetest thing that anybody had ever done for her in her life. She felt the world around her dissolve as she stared into Ryan's earnest, radiant eyes. "Do I look pretty?" she breathed.

Ryan nodded. "The most beautiful girl in the world." He lifted his hands and cupped Jade's face. "You're absolutely gorgeous," he added, before leaning forward and planting a kiss on Jade's lips.

Her first kiss. It was so gentle, so delicate, so soft, and it tasted like fresh peppermints. They might have kissed for a few seconds, or maybe a few hours, she wasn't sure, but it was the best feeling in the whole world.

When they broke off, Ryan took out a small device from his pocket.

"Jade," he whispered, gesturing at the button in the middle of the device. "Press this for me, won't you?"

Jade's head was still spinning from euphoria. "What is it?"

"It's a surprise."

"Okay." Jade giggled once more before pressing on the button. She looked up at Ryan eagerly. "What now?"

Ryan's smile twisted.

"Goodbye, Jade," he said. His warm, loving tone had completely disappeared; his piercing brown eyes were now filled with a strange, unexplainable mix of emotions.

Jade blinked. "What?"

And then Ryan vanished.

In a blink of an eye, Jade was alone in her garden. Her hands were still warm from Ryan's touch and the flower crown still tickled her on the head. But Ryan was nowhere to be seen.

Realization hit her; dread filled the bottom of her heart, followed by regret, then anger, then hopelessness.

Ah, so he did have a Gift, after all.

There was a loud roar behind her. She turned around, her feet trembling. In the horizons, a wave of fire was approaching her, burning everything it touched into ashes and dust. She watched as her town, her house, the hill, disappeared into tides of bright, golden flames.

A single tear streamed down her cheek. She really should've listened to the adults more —Earthlings are always an omen of death. Always.

She clutched onto the flower crown with her shaky hands. A hidden thorn poked into her hand, causing her to bleed, but she didn't even notice the pain. She closed her eyes and waited.

"Mom, Dad, I'm so sorry."

***

1

T he target bounced around the room in an unrecognizable pattern. In a split second, they were punctured with five holes, straight through the middle. Smoke sizzled from each perforation.

"Congratulations for completing advanced mode, Lara Skyborn." The neon words floated in front of the dismantled target. "Your result is: 98.5% accuracy."

Lara put down the pistol and let out a sigh. She needed even more practice; this result was slightly better than last week's, but it was still far, far away from Arianna's record of 99.9%. But for now, a well-deserved break. She wiped her sweat from her forehead and stretched her throbbing arms. Then, she made her way towards the cafeteria.

The cafeteria was spacious and bustling with trainees and Operatives. They were gathered among their own cliques, eating and chatting away. Round, fluorescent lights illuminated the place, reflecting off the white floorings and glossy tables. Lara noticed a few of her friends and waved amicably at them, before positioning herself under a dispenser.

"One soda, please," she called out. A bottle of soda fell out of a halo-like opening on the ceiling, and onto her outstretched hand. With a quick twist of the cap, she began to chug the drink.

"You know you don't have to be so polite when you're ordering from the bots, right?" A familiar voice chuckled behind her.

Lara was so excited she almost choked on some of the soda that had not yet made its way down her throat. "A- Arianna!" she spluttered, quickly spinning around and wiping her mouth. "You're back! How are you feeling?"

The middle-aged redhead laughed. "I'm recovered, mostly," Arianna said while she patted Lara's brown, silky hair that was carelessly pulled into a ponytail. "How have you been, Lara?"

"Pretty good! I've been training really hard," Lara said with a grin. It had been almost a month since she last saw her older friend. She was used to it though; the Operatives always needed time off to rest after using their Gifts, although Arianna had been taking unusually long breaks recently. "I just got a 98.5% accuracy in advanced mode, too! Soon, I'll surpass you, and I'll finally get myself a Gift."

"Looking forward to it." Arianna beamed; her gentle, ocean blue eyes squinted into the shape of a crescent moon. "And you'll get your Gift soon, I'm sure of it."

"You think so?" Lara's heart soared. Hearing this from one of the most powerful Operatives on Earth gave her confidence a much needed boost. "Oh, I really hope I get a Gift as cool as yours, Arianna.

Or maybe something like superstrength, or even laser eyes. Well, I'll be happy with whatever, as long as it's nothing like that guy's..."

Arianna raised her eyebrows knowingly as she tried to hide a smile. "Speaking of which, that guy just got back from his mission a few days ago. I saw him at the sick bay."

Lara scowled. He was back so soon already? She had been really enjoying the few weeks of peace and quiet during his absence. "Argh, let me guess, he failed the mission."

"No. He succeeded," Arianna said nonchalantly. "The realm of Paradys is terminated."

Lara blinked. "What? He actually... succeeded...?" she stammered. She felt as though someone had just slapped her in the face. Paradys was one of the most notorious Turned Realms; it was a realm so powerful that not even Arianna —the Master of the Winds, the Summoner of Hurricanes, the Weather Controller— could defeat. "How did that guy, that- that weakling, coward... How on Earth did he succeed... in Paradys... when even you couldn't..."

A sudden commotion at the entrance of the cafeteria jolted Lara out of her dazed ramblings.

"Aye, welcome back Ryan!" "Yo, congrats dude!" "Ryan, looking good!"

Lara turned around, trying her very best not to roll her eyes. And there he was, Ryan Carland, sashaying into the cafeteria with his signature smug look and annoying confidence. As people crowded around him, he greeted each of them with either a casual hand slap or waving finger guns.

The moment he noticed Lara, his grin widened and he made a beeline for her.

"Ah, there you are, baby Lara, I've been looking for you," he said with his usual aggravating smirk that made Lara's hands itch to punch him.

Lara glared at the man with the intensity of a thousand flying daggers. "I told you to stop calling me that."

"How can I stop when you are a baby?" Ryan teased Lara one more time before turning to Arianna and giving her a curt nod. "Arianna."

"Ryan." Arianna returned the gesture. "Congratulations on the mission, by the way, it's very impressive. How did you do it? Paradys had a phenomenal team of battlers."

Ryan put a hand in his pocket and ruffled his curly, brown hair with his other hand. "My Gift makes it easy to get past them." He shrugged.

"Why did they not just kill you before you're able to teleport back out?" Lara grumbled. That was a question she had every time Ryan was sent for a mission and managed to come back alive —his combat skills and physical strength were next to nothing, and his Gift of teleportation was so weak that he could only use it once before he needed days of rest and recovery.

"Easy," Ryan replied while wiggling his eyebrows. "I just scour the realm for someone like you to help me."

"What? What do you mean someone like me?"

"Naive, stupid, easily duped by a handsome man like me."

Lara could feel her face turning hot. "I am not stupid," she snapped, "and you are the ugliest man on Earth!"

Ryan chortled. "Whatever you say, little baby Lara."

"Stop calling me that!"

"I will once you get your Gift." He gasped dramatically. "Oh wait, you'll never get one. You're too dumb to be an Operative."

Lara lifted her clenched fist, ready to lunge at Ryan, when Arianna placed a hand on her shoulder. "Just ignore him, Lara," Arianna soothed. "You know he's just messing with you."

Arianna was right; all her life, Ryan had done nothing but teased her incessantly. It was as if he made it his life goal to make her as sad as possible, and doubt herself as much as possible. But it still didn't make his taunts any more bearable over the years.

She crushed up her empty bottle of soda. She could feel thousands of amused eyes fixated on her from all over the cafeteria, and her face flushed a brighter red. "Argh, seriously, how did someone like you get a Gift?" she spat before storming out of the cafeteria.

As she stalked back to the training room, she could still hear Ryan's mocking laughter echoing along the curved hallway. Whatever, she was going to take her anger out by shooting the hell out of the targets! After slamming the door open, however, she stopped dead in her tracks.

The First Lady was waiting inside the training room.

"M- Madam..." Lara managed to croak. She hurriedly wiped some of her tears away.

Elena was wearing her usual long, flowy gown. Her platinum blonde hair spilled down over her shoulders, back and chest like gentle waves of waterfall. Sitting on her head was a gold tiara molded into a shape resembling that of a flower crown. Shiny diamonds lined the tiara, while a bright green gem stood out in the middle, matching her beautiful emerald eyes. As Lara entered the room haphazardly, Elena gave her the usual serene smile she always wore.

"Hello, Lara, thought I'd find you here."

"Y- Yes!" Lara blurted, standing up so straight that she almost fell forward. "I'm- I'm training hard, per your request, Madam."

"I know, and I appreciate you for that." Elena strolled towards her with her hands clasped behind her back, a small smile never leaving her face. "Lara, my dear, you're turning eighteen really soon, right?"

"In- in a week."

Elena nodded, and then placed a hand on Lara's cheek. "Well then, I think it must be time," she whispered. "Time for you to get a Gift."

Lara was so stunned by this information that she suddenly forgot how to breathe. "A... A Gift? Madam, do you... do you really mean that?"

"Why, yes, of course." The green hues of Elena's eyes seemed to shimmer with amusement.

It took a while for Lara to fully comprehend the weight of that information. She did it, she actually did it... After years of hard work, she's finally getting a Gift. She took in a deep, shaky breath, before running towards the First Lady and hugging her tightly by the waist.

"Thank you, Madam, thank you so, so much! I've been waiting my whole life for this!" she cried.

"I know, I know." Elena held Lara up gently. "And I'm really sorry for making you wait so long for it. I was hoping to wait till you're a little bit older, you know? I don't want to send you out to missions before you become an adult."

"Madam, you were... just waiting for me to turn eighteen...?" Lara asked.

Elena chuckled and cupped Lara's face. "Yes, my dear. Remember what I told you before? You were born under a very special star, and therefore you are special to me. After getting your Gift, will you be my most loyal and bestest Operative?"

Lara knew that it was part of Elena's Gift that made people around her flutter with happiness, but at that moment, she was truly, truly happy. "Yes, I will, Madam," she declared. "I will be the one who will end all Turned Realms." A thought occurred to her, and she added, "But Ryan had a Gift even before he was eighteen." In fact, for as long as she could remember, Ryan always seemed to possess a Gift.

"Ah yes, Ryan's Gift is..." Elena's eyelashes quivered slightly. "A mistake."

A mistake? Lara almost laughed out loud. This was definitely something she could rub into that smug face of Ryan's the next time she sees him. "Can't you take it away from him?" Lara asked. After all, the First Lady had the ability to both grant Gifts and also take them away.

"He's been proving useful so far, so I'll let him keep his little Gift." Elena's smile faded away. "Lara, are you getting close to him?"

"Argh, hell no." Lara stuck out her tongue almost instinctively. "He's super annoying, and really mean to me, and he's always saying terrible things about-" The rest of the sentence got stuck in her throat.

Elena shot Lara an icy look. "About me?"

Lara instantly regretted what she blurted out. No matter how much she hated Ryan, she didn't really want him to get into trouble with the First Lady. "N... No, no!" she stammered. "He doesn't really say anything terrible about you, at most he'll... he'll just laugh at me a lot when I... when I praise you."

The anger in the First Lady subsided. "I know I can always count on you, Lara," she said, her smile returning to her face. "See you on your birthday for your birthday Gift, alright?"

"Y- Yes! Thank you, Madam!" With that, Lara rushed to open the door for the First Lady. To her surprise, the door swung open to reveal a sheepish-looking Ryan standing outside the training room.

"Ryan?" Lara was taken aback. The Operative never trained, ever, so why was he here?

"Hey, baby Lara," he greeted. His cheery smirk vanished when he noticed Elena standing behind Lara.

"Ryan." Elena peered at the man coolly. "May I know what you are doing here?"

Ryan returned Elena's gaze with an unwavering glare. "To train," he answered sharply. Ryan was possibly the only person in the entire universe —other than the people in the Turned Realms, of course— who dared to treat the First Lady with such an attitude.

Elena pursed her lips. "Tell the truth, Ryan." These words seemed to reverberate inside Lara's brain, sending chills down her spine. Madam's voice was like an echo of cold, dark energy coated with a layer of ice shards; this was the First Gift, and it was in its full effect.

Lara shuddered, and her eyes darted back to the Operative worriedly. She had never experienced the First Gift for real before, but she had seen it in effect a few times in her life. This would not turn out well...

The tall man's body tensed up. "I'm... I'm here to see Lara," he muttered through grinding teeth.

"What for?"

"To... apologize..."

Lara almost let out a sob. Ryan would have never admitted something like that, if not for the First Lady's Gift.

"Well, you shouldn't disturb her," Elena continued. "If you are here, you should train."

"Yes, Madam."

"And don't leave this room until you pass the intermediate level."

Ryan's eyes widened. For a millisecond, Lara could see fear flashe across his brown eyes. "...Y- Yes, Madam," he mumbled.

"Good." The First Lady gave him a satisfied smile before finally leaving the training room.

With only the two of them left, the square, metallic room became eerily quiet, and somehow even colder than normal. The paper targets lined along the end of the shooting range felt as though they were gawking at the two humans, especially at Ryan's misfortune.

Lara watched in exasperation as Ryan trudged towards the shooting range and activated the intermediate mode. She knew that the power of the First Gift was unrivaled, and so Ryan had to listen to Madam's orders no matter what. But there was no way Ryan could ever pass the intermediate level; he could barely even pass the beginner level!

"Do you... do you want me to help you with that?" Lara asked hesitantly.

"What, do you want to get punished too?" Ryan said without turning back to look at her. His demeanor was drastically different from just a minute ago at the cafeteria.

"N- No..." Lara sighed and folded her arms. "But you know, if you are just a tad bit more respectful to Madam, she won't do this to you. I've also made mistakes, or accidentally lied to her, but she has never punished me like this before."

Ryan didn't reply. He focused on setting up his pistol.

Lara was not used to the lack of retort or snide comment, and so she continued babbling, "I don't know why you always insist on being so disrespectful to her. She's the First Lady, you know, she deserves some respect. Without her, there wouldn't be any Gifts, and we'd still be stuck in the Grand War, where every realm is fighting and tearing one another apart. She's basically our savior."

Ryan didn't reply again. The training started, and the targets started to bounce all around the shooting range. Ryan took aim and shot. He missed every single one of them.

"I'm sorry, but you've failed intermediate mode, Ryan Carland." The words floated in front of Ryan, as if mocking him. "Your result is: 9.3%."

Lara snorted. "Wow, you really suck. You know, Madam just told me that your Gift was a mistake, and it makes so much sense now. I can't see how you can ever qualify for a Gift with skills like these."

Ryan glanced at Lara. "At least I have one and you don't."

Normally, this would have absolutely crushed Lara. Instead, Lara puffed her chest out proudly. "I'll have you know that I'm getting a Gift on my birthday."

"Oh." That seemed to have finally gotten Ryan's attention. "Congratulations," he said as he put down his pistol and stared at Lara with a very strange expression. Was it anger? Fear? Or maybe envy?

Lara took the chance to brag more. "Yeah, and I bet my Gift is going to be a thousand times better than yours. Apparently, I'm born under some kind of special star or something. I bet this means that my Gift is going to be super strong and super cool, unlike you and your lame teleportation Gift."

Ryan's eyes were still boring into Lara curiously. "Well, I don't doubt that," he admitted. "Looking forward to it."

"Wait, you are?" Lara frowned. Ryan was seriously acting very strange; she was expecting way more snarky remarks from him.

Maybe Elena's Gift had been preventing him from saying them, somehow.

Ryan nodded gravely, and then turned his attention back to the shooting range. Once again, Lara watched helplessly as he missed every single target in his next round.

***

2

L ara peeked her head into the sick bay. The modest room was cramped with a dozen beds separated by thin, light blue curtains. They were mainly occupied by Operatives, as well as some unlucky trainees. A few nurses were standing around with their clipboards, jotting down vital signs and whatnots.

As Lara scanned the room, she recognized a few Operatives, but Ryan was nowhere to be found.

Did he get discharged already? When Lara brought him here yesterday, all his fingers were blistered and bloody, and he was burning up so badly from exhaustion. It was already a miracle that he managed to pass the intermediate mode and made it out of the training room alive —how was he able to recover so fast?

Suddenly, Lara noticed a familiar figure at the far end of the packed room. "Arianna?" she asked incredulously. "Are you okay?"

The middle-aged redhead was equally taken aback. "Lara," Arianna said with a weak smile. She was sitting up on a bed, leaning against the pillow as if she had all her energy drained from her. "I'm okay, just doing a quick check-up. What are you doing here?"

Lara scratched her head. "I am, erm, trying to, well, check up on that jerk..."

"You mean Ryan?" Arianna chuckled. "I saw him. He left in the morning when I arrived. I don't think he was supposed to, though, but he mentioned something about needing a drink."

"Oh, of course." Lara rolled her eyes dramatically. "I bet he's going to the bars outside again."

"Does he do that often?"

"Yeah, he does." Lara snorted. "And he always laughs at me and calls me a baby when I ask him what's the appeal of bars. Seriously, what is the appeal of them? It's just alcohol and loud music. Whatever, he'd better come back before curfew, or his annoying butt is going to be punished again."

Then, Lara remembered something. "Oh right, I forgot to tell you!" she exclaimed, a wide grin appearing on her face. "It's my birthday today, and guess what? Madam is going to give me a Gift later!"

Arianna stared at Lara. "She is?" she mumbled. Her sky blue eyes looked as though a storm cloud had invaded them.

"Yeah!" Lara continued, unaware of Arianna's peculiar expression. "You were totally right, Arianna! Right after you told me I'll get a Gift, Madam came to tell me that I am getting it! Isn't it great-"

Lara stopped mid-sentence when Arianna lunged out of the bed and grabbed her hands harshly.

"A- Arianna?" she stammered. Her older friend was holding onto her like a desperate koala hanging onto a tree in the middle of a burning forest —her grip was shaky but firm, and her eyes were frantic with despair.

"Don't do it, Lara!" Arianna yelled. "Getting a Gift and becoming an Operative is the worst decision I have ever made in my life! Please, Lara, you have no idea what I've done, especially to you and R-"

Suddenly, she stopped. Her entire body slumped. "M- Madam," she whispered.

Hearing that, Lara spun around. Indeed, the First Lady was standing behind her, with her usual elegant gown and beautiful tiara. Under the white fluorescent lights of the sick bay, her platinum blonde hair glistened and shimmered, as if she had a halo around her head.

"Arianna." Elena gave the Operative a warm smile. "You've been visiting the sick bay so much, I'm starting to get worried."

Arianna hung her head. Her already pale face became even paler, somehow. "I'm sorry for worrying you, Madam..."

"Take care, alright? You're precious to me," Elena said as she smoothed Arianna's long, auburn hair. Then, she turned to the brunette who was still standing by the bed, frozen with shock. "Come with me, Lara. Let Arianna rest."

"Y- Yes, Madam," Lara muttered. She shot her friend a worried glance, before hesitantly following the First Lady out of the sick bay.

They trotted down the white corridor that encapsulated the entire building. It was bright, spacious, and lined with curved arcs and open windows. At the end of the corridor stood a wooden door that was lavishly decorated with gold and gemstones. Two Operatives stood guard on each end of the giant door. As Elena and Lara approached, they laboriously pushed the door open for them to enter.

It was the First Lady's office. A huge chandelier hung in the middle of a cavernous room. The sparkle from the glass drops illuminated the luxurious furniture and gold ornaments. Despite Lara having visited the room countless times, the opulent, Victorian-style decorations still hit her with fascination; it was such a stark contrast to the usual, plain facade of the rest of the building.

Elena settled comfortably on an arm chair and gestured for Lara to do the same. "So, are you ready for your Gift, Lara?"

Lara took a seat. "Madam, A- Arianna... She's... Is she..." she mumbled. The image of her distressed friend still burned in her mind. Arianna had always been the much older and wiser confidante she looked up to; she had never seen her this agitated and distraught before, ever.

"Arianna has been an Operative for fifteen years, Lara," Elena said with a small sigh. "She has seen too much and it's starting to weigh down on her."

"She's seen too much...? Do you mean... from her missions?"

"Yes." Elena nodded gravely. "After years of going into the Turned Realms and seeing what goes on down there, it definitely takes a toll on you."

"Is it..." Lara gulped. "Is it really that bad?"

Elena peered at Lara. "Of course, Lara, going to the Turned Realms is not for the faint-hearted. Do you remember the story I taught you?"

"Yes." Lara lowered her gaze and began to recite the story that she had heard almost every single day in her childhood. "Before the Gifts, the realms were constantly at war with one another, until the First Gift was granted to you. The First Gift represents the two virtues, Unconditional Love and Unwavering Faith, and with this Gift, you are able to grant Gifts to other people, as well as command deference. And you used this Gift to stop all wars and bring all the realms together.

"But evil still remained. People who still thirst for war and terror still exist, and they reign the realms that turned against you. We call them the Turned Realms, and not only do they long for our destruction, they bring suffering to their own people too. They are a reign of terror that needs to be stopped."

Elena smiled, extremely satisfied at Lara's well-trained answer. "Very good, Lara. The Turned Realms have existed for about fifty years now, but soon, we will terminate all of them." She stood up and walked over to Lara, placing her hand on the girl's hair. "With your help, of course."

Lara nodded and clenched her fists. This was it. This was everything that she had trained for for all her life. She was finally getting a Gift from the First Lady. She was finally becoming an Operative.

She recalled all the physical training she had to go through: the intense combat training, the shooting lessons, the weekly physical fitness test. She remembered all the grueling tests she had to sit through, the giant texts on the history of the First Lady that she had to memorize, the nightly revisions that Arianna supervised.

Arianna...

Lara's mind wandered to the days when she would camp outside the building, waiting for Arianna to come back from a mission. The older woman had so much energy then; she could fly herself down from the spaceship, smiling ear-to-ear as everyone cheered for her. Back then, she could even bring Lara to the fields and create rows and rows of hurricanes, as many as Lara wanted to see. Lara had wanted nothing more in life than to be just like Arianna.

She closed her eyes. This was it. She was ready.

"I'm ready, Madam. I'm ready to be an Operative." I'm ready to be just like Arianna.

"Very good." Elena's emerald eyes glinted with pride. "You are a very special girl, Lara, and I've been preparing you your whole life to become my new right-hand Operative. You will be the one to end the rest of the Turned Realms. You will become the next Arianna."

Lara blinked. What? Become the next Arianna? What did that mean? Arianna's Gift was essentially unrivaled by any other Operatives, so was her Gift going to be at the same level or something?

"I am going to give you Arianna's Gift."

Time seemed to stop at that moment. Lara stared at Elena, mouth agape. "What?" she blurted. "B- But... What about Arianna...?"

"Arianna has served me for fifteen years now," Elena said as she patted Lara's brown ponytail, "and now, it's time for her to rest."

Lara still couldn't believe it. Each Gift in the world was unique, so if Lara was given Arianna's gift, was Arianna... going to lose her Gift?

Elena continued nonchalantly, "You'll take over her as the most powerful Operative I have, Lara. And then, you'll help me end the last few Turned Realms, won't you?"

Lara's head was spinning, and she felt sick to her stomach. She had always wanted a cool Gift like Arianna's, to be a powerful Operative like Arianna, to grow up to be like Arianna... but she had never, ever, wanted to take Arianna's Gift!

But... maybe this was a good thing. Arianna had been gradually losing her cheerfulness and energy over the years, and recently, she looked unusually exhausted all the time. The missions seemed to be taking a bigger toll on her as she went on more of them. So... maybe it's a good thing that she's retiring? Maybe with this, Arianna could finally rest, and she didn't have to overexert herself or go to the sick bay anymore... And if this was what the First Lady deemed appropriate, then maybe this was the right course of action...

Slowly, she nodded.

"I'm ready."

Lara felt two palms resting heavily on her head. She heard the First Lady let out a deep breath. Then, a surge of energy ran through her, as if she had chugged three bottles of soda in one sitting, only without the bloatedness or the sugar rush.

She lifted her hands and looked at them. Tiny, bright blue sparks of electricity radiated from her fingers. Instinctively, she put her hands together and shaped them into a bowl. The air in her cupped palms spun around, creating a small ball of twisting wind. This was Arianna's Gift: the Master of the Winds, the Summoner of Hurricanes, the Weather Controller. The coolest Gift in the world.

And she took it from her.

This was supposed to be the moment that Lara had been waiting for all her life, but she couldn't bring herself to feel happy at all. Instead, a heavy lump of dread grew inside her chest.

Elena, however, was beaming with delight. "Congratulations, Lara," she said. "How do you feel?"

"I- I don't know..." Lara's mouth felt as though there were mud inside, bitter and sandy. "T- This is cool, I guess..."

"You're officially an Operative now." Elena settled back onto her armchair and crossed her leg. "Now, time for your very first mission."

"Already?"

"Yes, of course. Time to use your Gift for the first time." Elena turned her head and called, "Bring him in."

The two Operatives who were standing guard outside the room entered. They were dragging a boy in chains into the room. He looked around Lara's age, but had skin as dark as charcoal. As they pushed him to the ground, he whimpered a little, his brown eyes darted around the room in fear.

"This man is a spy from the Realm of Karz, one of the most influential Turned Realms out there," Elena explained calmly, "and he is your first mission. Use your new Gift and terminate him."

Lara stared at Elena, bewildered, and then at the boy, and then at Elena again. "W- What? But he's just... he's just a kid, Madam..."

Elena's gaze was cold and unwavering. "He's from a Turned Realm, Lara. He's a spy that was threatening our safety. Terminate him."

The Karzian boy started to cry, but his voice sounded as though they were stuck in his throat permanently. As much as his body was jerking hysterically, only soft, weeping sounds could be heard. Elena must have prevented his ability to speak; he could very well be trying to beg for mercy, but no one could hear them. Lara couldn't even bear to look at him anymore. His brown, shimmering eyes looked too much like the pair of eyes she saw everyday when she looked into the mirror.

"He's... he's harmless right now, why... why does he need to be killed...?" Lara stammered.

"Just do as I say, Lara."

"B- But, I... I don't..."

"Lara," Elena growled, her patience waning, "kill him."

The First Gift.

Lara's vision blurred with tears. Madam had never used her Gift on her, ever. After all, Lara had always been the perfect and obedient trainee, who had always listened to Elena's every command. But this was... this was too much... Lara had prepared herself to fight an army of ruthless, heinous, evil reincarnate from the Turned Realms, but this? A small, defenseless boy in chains? This wasn't what Lara signed up for at all...

"I- I can't..." Lara croaked, tears streaming down her face. "I can't do this, Madam..."

Everyone in the room turned to stare at Lara in disbelief, even the Karzian boy. It took a few seconds before it finally dawned on Lara as well: wait, the First Gift did not work on her!

What the hell?

"M- Madam, I- I don't know what happened..." Lara stuttered, staggering backwards in fear. "I just- I just can't do this... I don't know why, I..."

Elena was glaring at her with the coldest expression she had ever seen in her life —it was a look of utter hatred and pure anger. The expression was so horrifying that it shocked Lara to the core, and she started to tremble.

"Take her away," Elena snapped at the other two Operatives.

"Madam, please..." Lara cried. She tried to reach out her hands towards the First Lady, but before she could, her world turned black.

***

3

_____ eight years ago —

The moonlight peeked through the curtains, casting streaks of bright yellow on the off-white paper that Lara was writing on. Occasionally, blobs of water dripped onto the notebook, causing the messy handwriting to be even more unreadable.

The small girl hunched in front of the table, with her head lowered and brows furrowed in concentration. Her long brown hair was sprawled all over the mahogany table, like the twisting roots of a tree. She was trying her best to write, but it was difficult keeping her hand stable while sobbing.

"Why the hell are you crying?"

Lara's head jerked up towards the familiar voice. Perched on the windowsill, silhouetted against the full moon, was Ryan. He was leaning on his knee with one hand, and ruffling his short, curly hair with the other. When he locked eyes with the younger girl, his grin widened.

"Wow, you're honestly such a baby," he teased.

Lara quickly wiped her tears away. "Why are you here, you idiot?" she grumbled, embarrassed that the teenage boy caught her crying again. "If Madam finds out you're here, she'll punish you."

Ryan shrugged. "Whatever. Tell her then, I dare you."

"S- Shut up..." Lara pouted. Of course Ryan knew that she was never really going to snitch to the First Lady. "I- I'll tell Arianna instead."

Ryan snorted. "What can she even do to me? Strike me down with hurricanes? As if she has the energy to spare for that." Then, he hopped off the window and sauntered next to Lara. "What is this? What the hell are you writing?" he asked, snatching up the notebook on the table.

"Hey, give it back!"

The small girl tried to pounce on Ryan, but he effortlessly held her down with one arm. He squinted at the written words and scrunched up his nose. "Why are you writing about the Grand War?"

Lara sniffed. "M- Madam tested me today and I- I forgot the dates," she mumbled, her body still heaving a little from her sobs. "She- She told me to write the chapter fifty times by tonight."

Ryan peered at her curiously. "Screw her." He stuffed the notebook into his inner pocket of his jacket. "Go to sleep."

"What? I can't do that!" Lara exclaimed. Her tears started flowing down her face uncontrollably again. "Give it back, I- I have to listen to Madam, or- or else..."

"Or else what?" Ryan raised his eyebrows. "Or else she won't give you a Gift? Go look in the mirror right now, you look like an oversized baby, crying at the slightest thing. She's never going to give you a Gift, ever, so just give up."

"Shut up!" Lara screamed. "Madam said I'm destined to get it one day!" She summoned all the energy she had in her and jumped on Ryan, hitting his body and pulling on his jacket hysterically. That must have hurt Ryan to some degree, as he retaliated with a force much stronger than what he normally used for the smaller girl. With a hard push, Ryan shoved Lara right in the stomach, and she crashed right into the leg of her table. A sharp pain shot up her shoulders.

"Ow!" she yelped as she writhed in pain.

Ryan looked almost apologetic, but that expression immediately disappeared when Arianna barged into the room.

"What's happening?" the auburn-haired woman demanded. Her frown deepened when she noticed Ryan, but quickly softened when she saw the weeping Lara on the floor. "Oh Lara..." She knelt down next to the girl and gave her a tight hug. "It's okay, Lara, I'm here, it's all good now."

Ryan rolled his eyes. "Crybaby Lara."

Lara buried her head into Arianna's embrace. "Go away, Ryan! I hate you!"

"Yes, you should go back to your quarters, Ryan," Arianna added. "You know Madam doesn't want you around Lara. You don't want to anger her even more, do you, especially after your failed mission?"

"Mission?" Lara lifted her head and stared at Ryan. "You did a mission? Are you an Operative already?"

Ryan's deep brown eyes seemed to glaze over. "Yeah, she made me one the moment I turned eighteen," he admitted sourly.

"Oh." Lara could not comprehend Ryan's grimace. Becoming an Operative should be something to be celebrated, so why did he somehow look... pained? "How... How was it?"

"She fucking told you, didn't she? I failed," Ryan snapped. "What else do you want to know?"

"Language, Ryan," Arianna warned.

Ryan muttered a few more curses under his breath before walking away and climbing up the window.

"Hey!" Lara suddenly remembered. "Come back! Give me back my notebook!"

Ryan stuck out his tongue at Lara. "No," he said, and then, with a small leap, he vanished out of sight. The curtains fluttered with his exit, and the dazzling moonlight pierced into the room once again, blinding Lara's vision for a split second.

Lara squinted before turning to Arianna. "Why is he always so mean to me? He's only ever mean to me, too, he's not mean to his other friends."

Arianna chuckled. She gently smoothed Lara's messy hair. "Just try to avoid him, like I always say."

"I can't, he's always finding me." Lara groaned. Then, she sat up right enthusiastically. "Can I sleep with you tonight, Arianna?"

"Lara, you're a big girl now," Arianna chided with a feigned exasperated look. "You should sleep in your own room."

Lara continued staring at her older friend with beseeching eyes. "Could you read a story book to me, then?"

"Sure," Arianna relented.

Grinning, Lara leapt onto her bed, while Arianna tucked the blanket snugly around her. She listened to Arianna's soft and mellow narration of her favorite story, and watched the vividly blue eyes move along the pages of the book. Gradually, her eyelids grew heavier, and she drifted into dreams.

When she awoke, her notebook was placed next to her, all filled up with the words she needed to write.

— present —

Lara opened her eyes only to stare right into a blank, grey wall.

What the hell?

She tried to look around, but she quickly realized that she couldn't move an inch —her head, arms, torso, legs, every single part of her body, were all tightly bound to a chair. A soft whimper escaped her throat, and that was when she noticed that her mouth was stuffed with a ball the size of her fist. Slowly, she began to feel the discomfort in her jaw from having her mouth stretched out like that for... how long had it been?

Frantically, her eyes darted around the small room. As far as she could tell, she was just surrounded by walls. What used to be white paint was peeling off the surface. There was a narrow, horizontal window right below the ceiling, showing Lara a glimpse of the golden moon against a tranquil night sky. The sight was so beautiful that it seemed to be mocking her.

Was she... in prison? Lara tried to remember what happened before this. The image of the poor Karzian boy came to her mind and she immediately felt sick to her stomach. He had been in chains, shivering and staring at her with a set of sad, pitiful eyes... Had he also been tied up like this? Tears blurred her vision; she wanted to cry but her body was too restricted for her to let out a proper sob. And so, she just closed her eyes, and let her tears flow freely down her face.

"Jesus Christ, why are you always crying?"

Lara opened her eyes again and saw Ryan's head poking out from the small window. Desperately, she tried to call out to him, but she ended up with a muffled "Mmm! Mmm!!"

"Yeah, yeah, calm down, baby Lara," Ryan said. He laboriously cut down the metal frames on the window with a muted laser gun. After a few minutes, he managed to cut out enough space for him to squeeze through and get into the cell. He began to fiddle with the locks around Lara, starting with the one on her mouth.

The moment Lara could speak again, she admonished, "Ryan, what are you doing here? You'll get into trouble!"

The older man rolled his eyes. "I'm already in trouble. In case you haven't realized, baby Lara, whenever you're in trouble, I'm in trouble too."

"What do you mean?"

Instead of explaining, Ryan sighed and focused on picking the locks around Lara's body. "So, tell me, what the hell happened today? What did you even do to get yourself in this situation?"

Lara lowered her gaze. "Well... I got my Gift today," she muttered, "and Madam gave me Arianna's Gift."

Ryan stopped what he's doing to stare at her. "What the fuck? Seriously?" he asked incredulously. Then, he laughed. "Wow, no wonder you're all tied up like that, you're formidable now."

The rare praise from Ryan left a bad taste in her mouth. She got herself a powerful Gift, but at what cost? "I think Madam probably took it away by now..."

Ryan snorted. "If she did then she wouldn't have bound you up like you're ready to blow up the entire place. The security out there is insane too, I've never seen anything like it." He glanced at Lara before resuming his task. "So anyway, what happened after she gave you that Gift?"

Lara's hands were set free at this point. She rubbed her arms uneasily. "She gave me a mission on the spot, but I... couldn't do it."

"Yeah, not surprising, you're a baby after all." Ryan's low voice came from behind her. "What did she tell you to do?"

"She..." Lara's eyes fluttered. "Madam told me to kill this... this Karzian spy... on the spot..." She gulped. Her saliva tasted sandy and metallic. "But he was just a kid, Ryan, and I... I couldn't bring myself to do it..."

Ryan snorted again. "Of course she did that, what a fucking psycho."

Lara turned her face to observe the dark-haired man. "Did you... Did you also have to do something like that when you first got your Gift from Madam?" she probed warily.

"Nah. I didn't get my Gift from her."

"What?" Lara frowned. "Where did you get it from?"

"From myself."

This time, it was Lara's turn to roll her eyes. "Liar."

The only person who had ever spawned a Gift on their own was the First Lady. That was the reason why the First Gift was so powerful; every other Gift was technically derived from it, and thus could never come close to its sheer level of strength, potency, and stamina. While Arianna and Ryan had to carefully ration the usage of their Gifts and plan sufficient rest times in between each use, Elena had no such issue. She could freely use her Gift whenever and wherever with no repercussions to her body, and it would always work with a hundred percent effectiveness.

... Until Lara, of course.

"Oh right, Madam also used her Gift on me too, for the first time," Lara admitted dejectedly.

There was a short pause before Ryan whispered, "Did she force you to kill the kid?" His voice was unusually strained.

"S- She tried to..." Lara croaked, fighting back more tears. "But her Gift didn't work on me for some reason."

Once again, Ryan had to stop what he's doing. He poked out his head from behind her to stare at her in utter disbelief. "What?"

"Yeah, it was really strange. Maybe she wasn't really using it? Or maybe she's tired after granting me a Gift? I'm not sure."

Ryan scrutinized Lara in silence for a long time, a mix of emotions running through his face. When he finally managed to find his voice again, his tone took Lara by surprise —it was soft, gentle and sorrowful, unlike anything Lara had ever heard from this man in her entire life.

"Oh my God, Lara, it really is you," he breathed. "You really are our new Hope."

Lara blinked. "What? What do you mean?"

By now, Ryan was done with releasing all of Lara's shackles. He immediately stood up, grabbed her by the shoulders and pulled her in for a tight hug.

"I should've believed in you more. I'm sorry, Lara."

Lara was so shocked by this gesture that she couldn't even make a sound, except maybe a hushed and confused "W- What?"

After a long while, Ryan let her go and took out his phone. He played around with the maps app, zooming and swiping around an unknown location, his brows furrowed in deep concentration.

Lara had never seen the tall man this way before. Ryan had always acted so casual about everything in life, like he had never taken anything seriously. But right now, he's staring at his phone as if his life depended on it.

"What... What are you doing, Ryan?" Lara asked.

"I'm going to atone for my sins," Ryan replied gravely. When he seemed satisfied with the location that he found, he looked up and gave Lara a small smile. "It'll be okay, Lara. Listen to me, when you get there, tell them that you are the descendant of Elissa Skyborn, and that you are born under the star of Nadia. Then, tell them about what happened, about how Elena's original Gift didn't affect you at all. Promise me, make sure they know all that before they try to kill you, okay?"

Lara sighed in exasperation. "What on Earth are you talking about, Ryan?"

Ryan chuckled. "Not on Earth, baby Lara, not anymore."

Then, he grabbed her hands, and the entire world around her swirled into dark shadows, like they were sucked into some kind of vacuum. It was as if she had plunged into complete blackness —it felt so empty and so alone. But Ryan's warm hands, firmly wrapped around hers, kept her from spiraling into anxieties.

When the world appeared around her again, she found herself inside an unfamiliar room. Marbled pillars held up a ceiling that seemed almost as high as the sky. Giant oil paintings lined the well-lit, minimalistic walls. The walls were white and glossy, but it had a much warmer feel to them than back in their building on Earth.

However, Lara didn't have much time to admire the place, as Ryan let go of her hand and collapsed on the spot.

"Ryan!" she cried. She wanted to get down to help him, but a sword swung in front of her.

"Prepare to die, Earthling."

***

4

The long, curved blade blinded Lara for a millisecond, but she quickly shifted her focus towards the wielder of the sword —a lean boy who looked not much older than her. He had skin as light as Lara's but with a rosier undertone, and his monolid eyes were glaring at Lara with such animosity, as if she had murdered his entire family.

Most importantly, Lara noticed that he had a very unstable fighting stance. His feet were flat on the ground, his knees were straight as a stick, and he was holding onto the katana like a baseball bat. The first thought that came to Lara's mind was: oh, this should be an easy one.

Remembering her training, Lara swung her arms and gave the boy's wrists a brisk, sharp slap. His sword flew out of his hands and landed a few feet away, bouncing around with a few loud and humiliating 'clang, clang, clang'. With a sweep of her leg, she tripped the boy over, twisted his hands to the back, and kneed him firmly to the ground.

"Ow! Ow! Ow!" The dark-haired boy squirmed under her weight. Despite being bigger than Lara and having a weapon, he was basically powerless against her. It was obvious that he had not been trained.

Lara didn't have time to gloat, however. Her body froze in place when she felt several muzzles pressed into the back of her head.

"Stand up and put your hands behind your head," a low and husky voice commanded.

Lara cursed silently. There was no way she could ever fight her way out of this. Reluctantly, she followed the orders. The strange boy took the chance to scramble away, not forgetting to spit at Lara's face indignantly the moment he was out of arm's reach. Ah she really should've given him a punch in the face while she could...

"Turn around slowly," the deep voice continued, "and if you try anything funny, any sign of a Gift at all, we'll blast your head off."

Lara shuffled her feet cautiously and found herself standing in front of a row of soldiers clad in boxy, dark grey uniform, their rifles pointing at her. At a quick glance, they looked as though they were all from different realms; some of them had similar features to the boy who attacked her, others were slightly more tanned with sharper features, while a few people, including the tall, burly commander in the middle, had dark charcoal skin like the imprisoned Karzian boy. Whatever realms they might be from and whatever their skin color was, it seemed that they had one unifying goal in mind: to kill both Lara and Ryan. The cursed Earthlings.

Warily, Lara shifted a little bit to the side, blocking Ryan's unconscious body with her own. "W- What do you people want?" She tried to sound as intimidating as possible, but her voice came out as a meek squeak.

"What kind of question is that? You teleported here!" the dark-haired boy snapped.

"Jun, go to the back, and stay there," warned the commander. Jun grumbled a little to himself before retreating behind the rest of the soldiers.

The commander was a head taller than almost everyone in the room, and his uniform, taut against his bulging muscles, had additional badges on his collar and shoulder straps. Despite his steely expression, he had a pair of gentle brown eyes that matched his ebony skin —eyes that were very similar to those of the imprisoned Karzian boy, Lara noted. Just a thought of that poor boy made her heart ache once again.

"So I see that Ryan Carland, the notorious Operative, has brought you here. This is very unexpected of him. He knows very well that coming here would mean his death. Yet he still comes, and even brings you along. Why is that?"

Lara's mind had been inundated with questions ever since Ryan had transported them here, but she perked up when she heard the word 'death'. "I- I don't know, but- but please, don't kill him!"

"You are not in the position to be demanding anything from us, Earthling," the commander said, his brows furrowed. "Tell us, who are you?"

"I'm L- Lara." Then, Lara remembered what Ryan had told her. "Oh, erm, I'm- I'm apparently the descendant of erm..." —What was the name that Ryan had said again?— "Erm, Lisa Skyborn?"

"Elissa Skyborn?" A strange expression took over the commander's face. Everyone in the room also became visibly flustered at the mention of that name.

Did she get the name wrong? What else had Ryan told her to say? "Oh yeah, I'm- I'm born under a special star? The star of Nada, or something?" Lara tried to babble as much as she could remember. Ryan had not given her enough time to process before taking her here, so her memory was fuzzy at best. "And oh, Madam's- I mean, our First Lady's Gift didn't affect me at all, too..."

To Lara's surprise, the commander dropped his weapon on the ground. "Finally." He approached Lara and snatched up her hands endearingly. "After fifteen years, finally, that bastard returned you to us. We've been waiting for you, Lara."

"What?" The sudden change in attitude was giving Lara whiplash. "What do you mean?"

The commander's mouth bent upwards, revealing the kindest smile Lara had ever seen. "Come with me, Lara. Let's talk." With a casual wave of his hand, every other soldier lowered their weapons as well.

"O- Okay..." Lara glanced at Ryan, who was still lying on the floor. "But what about him? Please, don't hurt him."

"Lara, this man is responsible for the deaths of millions," the burly man said somberly. He lowered his voice and added with a whisper, "Including the death of your parents, Lara."

"What? What are you talking about?" Lara exclaimed. "Arianna told me my parents died when giving birth to me. And Ryan is an Operative, he only kills the ruthless armies of the Turned Realms."

Whatever Lara said caused quite a stir; some people cringed outwardly, while others, Jun included, began to cuss out loud. The room quietened down once again when the commander lifted his hand up.

"My child, is that what you think of Operatives? Some kind of knights of justice?" The commander looked as if he had just swallowed a mouthful of bitter medicine.

"Aren't they?" Lara insisted. "They kill the evil people who are working to destroy the peace in the universe."

A small sigh escaped the commander's nose. "Well, whatever you believe in, you have to remember that you are in our realm now, and therefore he is subject to our law. We will give him a fair and proper trial tomorrow, where we will decide on a punishment that he deserves. I'm sure it will be a punishment that you'll agree with as well, once you hear about what he's actually done." He nodded his head at two soldiers on the side. "You two, take him away."

Lara couldn't argue with that. The commander was right; she's no longer on Earth anymore. She watched helplessly as Ryan was dragged away from the room, his curly, brown hair mopping the stone-tiled floor. "What... realm am I in?" she asked, finally taking some time to look around the luxurious, palace-like room. What realm was this affluent, and had such diversity among their people?

"The realm of Karz."

Lara almost choked on her own saliva. "K- Karz? T- This is a Turned Realm?" She spun her head around a few more times again. From everything she'd heard from Madam, this was... not at all what she imagined a Turned Realm would look like.

"What, do we not look as evil as you think we are?" The commander chuckled. "Don't worry, Lara, we won't hurt you if you don't hurt us. Also, allow me to properly introduce myself. My name is Arthur Canary, and I'm the General Commander of the Karzian Army." He gestured to two soldiers who stood right behind him. "And these two are Nick and Yvo. They're my lieutenants. Come, walk with me, Lara, let's talk."

Hesitantly, Lara followed Arthur out of the room, with his two lieutenants trailing close behind. The rest of the army scattered as well, while Jun sheepishly went to retrieve his fallen sword. As Lara walked by him, he stuck up his middle finger out at her, and she felt no qualms in returning the obscene gesture.

The hallways were lined with the same exquisite marble pillars. In between each pillar, oil paintings or sculptures decorated the walls. Lara figured that this place was not really a palace, but probably some kind of a government building. A bunch of people clutching briefcases and wearing sophisticated office wear trotted along the corridors. They were as diverse as the soldiers in the room.

Whenever they noticed Lara, however, they would stop dead in their tracks and stare at her, like she was the literal spawn of the devil. Lara had never felt so... aware of her Earthling features —her porcelain skin stood out like a sore thumb in this realm. Arthur strode next to Lara, nodding his head calmly at the nervous passersby. His sheer presence was enough to placate any distress that Lara apparently caused.

"So Lara, how much do you know about the Turned Realms?" Arthur asked. "What exactly do you think we are?"

Lara hung her head. "I- I was told that... the Turned Realms were reigned by people who thirst for war and terror."

"Now, why would we want that?"

"I don't know." Lara looked up at the dark-skinned commander. "Is it not true?"

"Of course not." Arthur peered at the girl. "War is painful for everyone. Nobody wants to fight to the death ever."

"Then why would you turn against the First Lady? She stopped the Grand War and brought peace to the entire universe. Why would you want to go against that?"

Arthur nodded. "Yes, Elena did participate in stopping the Grand War, and I appreciate her for that. But you know, she didn't do it alone. There were others who were also granted the First Gifts."

Lara blinked. "Wait, what?"

"Ah, you don't know, do you?" Arthur said with a knowing smile. "She must have been omitting that information and taking the credit all by herself."

"What information?"

"The truth about how the Grand War ended."

By now, the two of them had arrived at the entrance of the building. Right outside the building was a roundabout circling a giant fountain. Dozens of limos parked along the side, their glossy surfaces sparkling in the sunlight. Arthur led Lara down the spacious pedestrian pathway next to the roads. Bougainvillea of all shades of red flanked the cobblestone pavement; the picturesque scenery and the pleasant weather was a drastic contrast to their topic of discussion.

"What do you mean?" Lara asked.

"Well, as you probably already know, the Grand War that occurred over a century ago was extremely unfortunate," Arthur said as they strolled down the pavement. "It happened as a result of unchecked power: many realms had leaders with so much pride, such that they let their egos make the decisions. Their race to become the powerhouse and overall leader of the universe escalated into unimaginable destruction. But right before any weapons of mass destruction were launched, we were granted with a blessing to stop all of that."

"I know that. It's the First Gift," Lara added. She had learnt all of this history by heart. "It was granted to the First Lady Elena."

"Not quite." Arthur raised his eyebrows. "There were actually three Gifts, and they were granted to three people. Elena was only one of them."

"Three?"

"Yes, specifically, the three sisters, Emilia, Elissa, and Elena Skyborn."

Lara stared at Arthur incredulously, her mouth wide open. The burly commander was not surprised by her reaction, and continued nonchalantly, "The three sisters each received a Gift that represented a virtue. They were Unconditional Love, Untrodden Hope and

Unwavering Faith. The Gift of Unconditional Love was the ability to grant Gifts to anybody at any capacity, and it was given to Emilia, the oldest sister. The Gift of Untrodden Hope was the ability to develop a Gift within oneself on demand, and it was given to Elissa Skyborn. Lastly, the Gift of Unwavering Faith was the ability to demand absolute loyalty from people, and it was given to Elena, the youngest sister.

"A hundred years ago, these three sisters came into existence and stopped the Grand War once and for all. They acted as peacemakers, guiding the realms to work together, uniting the realms as one harmonious universe. But that was all that they're meant to do: peacemaking. Elena, however, wanted more than that. Perhaps it was that she was the youngest sister, or perhaps it was that people were always so afraid of her and her Gift, but she became angry and dissatisfied at the altruistic nature of their job. She wanted more, she wanted to become the leader of the universe, to have the ultimate say in how the world was run, forgetting that that was the exact reason why the Grand War was even started.

"Emilia opposed the idea, of course. But then, fifty years ago, Elena used her Gift on her. She forced Emilia to grant her a Gift: a Gift that can take away other people's Gift. Elena then used this new Gift to take away Emilia's Gift for herself, so that she can possess the Gift of the oldest sister, the Gift that people admired the most."

Lara's head began to spin. The information was so appalling, and so different from what she grew up learning, but somehow, it clarified certain doubts that Lara always had. Elena's Gift had been very perplexing —each human can only be granted with one Gift, but Elena seemed to have more than just one.

"She killed her own sister just so that she can reign the universe." Arthur's low, husky voice trembled slightly. "Then, she proceeded to take away everyone's Gift; anybody who had been granted a Gift by Emilia had their Gift stripped away and handed to Elena's soldiers, or Operatives, as you call it. These cursed Operatives helped her continue her reign of terror."

He turned to look at Lara; his dark brown eyes were shimmering in the sunlight, as if they had been rinsed with tears too often. "And that, my child, is the true reason why the Turned Realm exists. We oppose Elena's rule, not because we want war for the sake of it, and not because we are the embodiment of evil that you've been taught. It is because she is not supposed to be using her Gift to rule the universe. And most of all, she is not the rightful owner of the very First Gift, the Gift of her oldest sister: Unconditional Love."

They reached the end of the pavement, arriving at a tall, arched gate. Across the polished metal bars was a row of two-storeyed shop-houses; each building had their own distinct color, ranging from pastel pink to bright orange, that complemented one another beautifully. In front of the shops were crowds of people as diverse as the soldiers and office workers in the building. The scene in front of Lara looked just like those old pictures of Earth she used to see in her history textbooks: the pictures of Earth before the existence of realms, before the invention of space travel.

But Lara was in no mood to admire this view. Her heart was beating so fast that she could barely hear the agitated murmurings of the shoppers and passersby as they walked by her. Elena's ability to grant wishes was... stolen? And so was every Operative's Gift? Just like how... she stole Arianna's? She clenched her fists to stop her hands from shaking.

"What- What about the second sister?" Lara whispered. "What about Elissa?"

"Ah, Elissa Skyborn has always been the most inconspicuous sister." Arthur's benign smile appeared again. "Right after the Grand War ended, she left to a faraway realm and started her own family. She was the only one of the three sisters who chose to let old age take her, and so she allowed her Gift to be passed along to her children. She passed it to your father, Marco, who was my very good friend."

"My father? You knew my father?"

"Oh yes, I did." Arthur let out a wistful laughter. "He was a kind and courageous man. And very talented at tennis; I could never beat him, and he never stopped rubbing it in my face about it."

Lara chuckled along too, but, for some reason, she felt tears well up in her eyes. Arianna had always avoided talking about her parents, and she had never thought to press. But to finally realize that some people actually knew who her parents were, and what they were like, made her heart swell.

"Fifteen years ago," Arthur continued, his eyes downcast, "your father and a whole team of us prepared for a raid to overthrow Elena. However, we were betrayed by... some of our own people..." His voice faltered, and he took in a deep breath to calm himself. "We failed the mission, and Bernu, your home planet where you were born, was terminated. Everyone else did not make it... including your parents...

"Undeservingly, I was the only one who survived, because I withdrew from the mission at the last minute. When I tried to find you, though, I realized that you were taken away by Elena. I thought that all hope was lost, but now, now you're back." He turned to face Lara, his expression solemn yet hopeful. "Lara, your father had always wanted you to be the next bearer of Elissa's First Gift. You were born under the Star of Nadia, which means that your Gift will be the strongest of them all. Seeing that Elena's First Gift stopped working on you further proves how powerful you are."

Arthur placed his hands on Lara's shoulders. "You are our new Hope, Lara, the daughter of Marco Carland, the rightful descendant of the Gift of Untrodden Hope."

Wait... Marco... Carland? Lara realized with a jolt that that was the same last name as Ryan's. "Am I... Am I related to Ryan?" she asked.

Arthur's face contorted into a bitter grimace. "Let's not speak of that scum of a man," he growled. Then, he motioned to his lieutenants. "Nick and Yvo will now escort you to a hotel. Have a good rest, Lara, and I look forward to seeing you tomorrow, at that traitor's trial."

He gave Lara one last smile before marching back towards the building by himself. Lara squinted her eyes as she watched him leave. Sunlight scorched his body, and his skin seemed to glisten like the beginning of a twilight before a sunrise. But Lara's heart, on the other hand, had sunk into the darkest of the night.

Ryan... What exactly have you done?

***

5

Lara stared blankly at her plate of breakfast. The two sunny-side up eggs seemed to stare right back at her like a pair of curious, googly eyes. She really should eat something; she had not eaten anything since coming here, or since being rescued by Ryan, or since getting her Gift from Elena...

She sighed and slowly took a bite of her toast. The small piece of bread sat inside her mouth idly, waiting to be chewed and swallowed, but Lara did not have the mood nor the energy to do any of that.

It did not help that she had been stuck in her hotel room since the day before. She had wanted to go out for a walk to clear her mind, and maybe to see what Karz was like, but whenever she tried to leave her room, the few people she met in the hallway would be scared out of their wits. One of them even passed out in fear.

And so, she remained in her room and resorted to people watching from her window. Everyone outside was walking about freely, chatting with their friends, drinking coffee by the patio. Lara was smelling foods she's never tried before, listening to languages she's never heard before, and seeing people from realms she's never been to. This place was so different from the strict, homogenous environment she grew up in. It was so carefree and lively, and so... captivating.

Time and time again, she had been told that places like Karz were a reign of terror that needed to be destroyed, but, as she peered enviously outside her window, she realized that that was obviously not true. On the other hand, the terrified expressions and looks of pure horror from the Karzians she met lingered in her mind. It turned out that she was the true terror.

How much of her life was a lie? How much of the truth was kept from her? And why?

Lara lifted her hands. The air above her palms twisted together, while sparks of lightning zapped across her fingers. She stared at the tiny tornado in disbelief —wait, she still had Arianna's Gift! Why wasn't it taken away? Did Elena's Gifts just... completely stopped working for her somehow?

Thinking of Arianna, she felt a squeeze in her heart. She missed her older friend so much. If Arianna had been here, she would've definitely been able to comfort her. She would've said something really sensible and wise, or at least given her a tight hug to make her feel better.

And, as much as she hated to admit it, she also really missed Ryan. He probably would've been annoying as usual, but he would've at least kept her mind from spiraling. She could already imagine his smug face and eye rolls, how he'd snort at her and say, "I told you so, baby Lara, the First Lady is a psychopathic bitch."

But seriously, what's going to happen to Ryan?

The saliva-soaked bread slid down her throat; it was lumpy and bitter, and almost made her gag. She buried her head into her hands. Despite her empty stomach, she still felt like puking.

Just then, the door slammed open. It was Jun, that rude boy from yesterday.

"You," he growled through gritted teeth, as if it was tortuous for him to speak. "Let's go." Without even waiting for a reply, he spun around and left.

Lara was so stunned by this sudden visitor that she sat frozen on her chair for a while, before realizing that he must be the new escort for her. She quickly dashed out of her room and followed him.

As expected, Lara caused quite a commotion in the streets. In addition to the horrified stares and startled gasps, a few onlookers spat out their coffee, while some joggers tripped over their feet. Embarrassed, she tried her best to stay as close to Jun as possible, but the boy was walking so fast, it was like he was actively trying to avoid her. Whenever she managed to catch up to him, he would increase his speed even more. After ten minutes of practically chasing each other, Lara had enough.

"Hey, slow down!" she called out. "What's your problem?"

Jun did not even bother looking at Lara as he snapped, "I was told to escort someone like you, that's what!"

"What do you mean by that?" Lara demanded. "What, do you not like it when a girl beats you?"

That finally got Jun to stop walking. He glared at Lara, his face turning a deep shade of red. "You're disgusting and cruel and horrible, just like all Earthlings!"

"Hey! Not- Not all Earthlings!"

Jun rolled his eyes and stomped off at an even faster pace than before, somehow.

Lara suddenly felt really bad. She shouldn't have said that, should she? She rushed over next to the dark-haired boy. "Hey, I'm- I'm sorry about... what we've been doing. I- I also only just found out yesterday about- about the truth... about Ma- the First Lady. I'm really sorry, but I never knew-"

"You work for her, you're essentially the same." Jun cut her off bitterly. "Fucking monsters trained to kill."

Lara could not reply to that. It was true, she really was trained to kill. Not only was she trained physically to kill, she was also given a Gift that was probably made to kill, too. Once again, she noticed the expressions of the passersby around her; they were all avoiding her as if she was death itself. Her jaw clenched; she had never felt so revolted by herself.

She decided to change the topic. "So, uh... Where are you from, Jun?"

Jun did not seem particularly happy with her attempt at a conversation. "What kind of question is that?"

"S- Sorry, I wasn't sure if you were from Karz originally," Lara mumbled, giving the sulking boy a few nervous glances. "You look very different from Arthur, that's why I asked."

"Are you stupid? Technically, no one is from Karz originally. We were all from Earth a long time ago!"

Lara huffed. "I knew that!" she lamented. "But that was like, centuries ago. You know what I really mean."

Jun rolled his eyes again, but his face softened. "I was born in Bernu. You know what happened there."

"Oh." Lara was taken aback. That was the realm that Arthur had mentioned. "I'm- I'm so sorry."

"A lot of people here also used to be from other realms, you know. Some of them were from Turned Realms that were destroyed and so they're here as refugees. Some were from other realms under Elena's rule, but are here for a better life." He glared at her, as though he was blaming Lara for all of this. "I don't know how you are all doing on Earth, but Elena is a really, really terrible ruler. Realms don't do well under her rule."

Lara lowered her head. "I'm- I'm sorry, I didn't know..." It seemed that she really didn't know a lot of things. She had grown up in a bubble, confined within the First Lady's headquarters. She had only known Elena as her teacher and mentor, and her only friends were Operatives or trainees preparing to become Operatives. How were the other people on Earth doing? She wasn't even sure of the answer herself...

"Because of you Earthlings, I lost my parents in Bernu fifteen years ago," Jun grumbled, his jaw clenched and his voice shaky. "I don't even remember what they look like now."

"Well, same with me, then," Lara whispered.

This time, it was Jun who was taken aback. "Really?"

"Yeah. Arthur told me yesterday that my parents died in Bernu too. Apparently Bernu is also my home planet."

Jun looked her up and down skeptically, but then blushed and quickly turned away. "I'm sorry about that too," he mumbled softly.

"It's okay, I don't remember them at all anyway. It didn't even cross my mind that they actually existed until yesterday. I mean, I've always had Arianna, she was basically my mother, even if she didn't like to admit it."

"Who's Arianna?"

"She's..." Lara's voice faltered. "Well, she's an Operative, but she's a really kind person, I swear! Well, at least, at least to me..." She noticed Jun's darkened expression and changed the topic again. "Anyway, what about you? Did you grow up in Karz?"

Jun nodded. "Arthur raised me."

"That's nice. He seems like he'd be a really good father."

Jun's mouth twitched a little, but the small smile disappeared almost immediately. "You don't even know him."

They walked down the same path that Lara took with Arthur yesterday. Visiting bees buzzed around the fragrant bougainvillea along the pavement; they were especially dewy in the morning fog. As they neared the government building, Lara noticed there was a crowd of soldiers and other officials gathered around the entrance, with more pouring in from newly arrived limos. Standing in the middle and towering over everyone was Arthur, who was talking to some people with a frown on his face. When he spotted Jun and Lara, he broke into an amicable smile and gave them a cordial wave.

Lara waved back, but decided not to bother him. "There's a lot of people," Lara said to Jun. "Are they all here for Ryan's trial?"

"It's a trial of the century, what do you think?" Jun replied curtly before heading into the building. "I really hope that bastard gets the freaking death sentence or something."

Lara pursed her lips and followed him silently. It seemed that everyone here really hated Ryan. Well, she did too, but she didn't want anything bad to happen to him. That guy was the most annoying, arrogant, condescending piece of shit who loved to bully her and make her cry at every single encounter, but... they still grew up together. The last thing she wanted was his death.

They entered a large, spacious courtroom that was already bustling with people. Rows of wooden benches filled the gallery, while large oak pillars held up a balcony with even more audience seating. A giant sculpture hung from the wall, looming over the entire room, as though it had emerged from the concrete to observe the trial. It was Lady Justice; a stoic, blindfolded woman holding up a scale on one hand, and a sword on the other. Despite the covered eyes, the statue seemed to be staring right into Lara's soul disapprovingly. Lara gulped and averted her gaze from it.

It took a while for everyone to slowly stream into their seats. Lara and Jun settled somewhere at the back, while Arthur strode all the way to the front, his two lieutenants trailing behind him. When the chamber door opened, the room turned eerily quiet. The judge walked into the room, followed by a few police officers, and, lastly, Ryan.

When Ryan appeared, Lara almost let out a scream.

He was covered in bruises; some were black and blue, while others were of a fresh, bright red color. Blood was still trickling out of his crooked nose and the scratches all over his face. One of his eyes was so swollen that it could not open, while his messy, curly hair had part of it yanked off. With handcuffs around his hands, he sauntered onto the witness stand, and then plopped down on the chair.

Lara covered her mouth with her trembling hands. Tears flowed down her face uncontrollably. She wanted to cry out in anguish, but her throat seemed to be blocked with phlegm. She couldn't make a sound; she could barely even breathe.

"Oh wow, he definitely did not have a good time in jail," Jun said with a dry laugh. He noticed Lara's distress and immediately refrained from commenting further.

Ryan, on the other hand, was scanning the room nonchalantly, his signature smug look still plastered all over his battered face. When he managed to lock eyes with Lara, he grinned and mouthed "baby Lara". Somehow, that made her tears flow even more.

The judge slammed her gavel and then peered down at Ryan. "The defendant, Ryan Carland, is charged with the destruction of six realms, Paradys, Honnu, Garjel, Vinris, Orolma and Pazon, as well as the first degree murder of approximately nine hundred and sixty million people from these realms. He is also charged with second degree murder of approximately two hundred and thirty-two million people from the realm of Bernu, due to his involvement in the rebellion fifteen years ago. How do you plead?"

Lara's jaw dropped. And then it dropped even more when Ryan, very indifferently, said, "Yeah, guilty as charged."

The courtroom broke into agitated murmurs. The judge had to slam her gavel a couple of times for the room to be silent. "The defendant has chosen to not contest his charges. You are now given the opportunity to provide any explanation or any special circumstances that would lessen the charge. Do you wish to say anything before sentence is imposed?"

"Nah, I'm good." Ryan shrugged. This action was so controversial that the room exploded into another round of noisy discussions.

At this point, Lara's mind went into a frenzy. What the hell was this guy thinking? Did he even know the severity of the situation he's in? In spite of her shaking legs and blocked windpipe, she bolted upright and screamed, "Ryan, you idiot! Now is not the time for you to be acting cool!"

Everyone in the room went silent once again; every pair of their eyes bored into the Earthling girl. Jun tugged at her shirt and whispered frantically, "Hey, sit down, you're not allowed to do this!"

Lara ignored him. "He's- He was ordered to terminate the realms!" she shrieked. "Please, it's not his fault at all! First Lady Elena used her Gift on him!"

"Would the defendant like to add a few words about that?" the judge asked.

Ryan looked at Lara, his eyebrows raised as if mocking her. "Nah, she's stupid, don't listen to her."

Lara wanted to retort, but the judge slammed her gavel. "The defendant has admitted to his charges. As such, Ryan Carland is guilty as charged. Following Karzian Penal Code 453B and Intergalactic Law Section Three Code 620A, I hereby sentence Ryan Carland to the death sentence for his crimes."

For the last time, the courtroom erupted. Loud chatterings, exclamations, and cheers filled the air. Some people were giving each other high-fives, while a few others even stood up for a standing ovation. The mood in general was hopeful and buoyant —justice prevailed, and was finally served.

Lara, on the other hand, slumped onto the bench, her face wet and sticky against her quivering hands. The whole world seemed to be spinning, and the pounding of her heart drowned out all the sounds around her. Slowly, her vision faded into an empty white, and she realized: she was all alone. All by herself, lost and floating in this unfamiliar realm, meaningless, powerless, helpless.

She had no one.

She was six. Her ice cream had fallen onto the ground. She was kneeling over it, sobbing. It was the only treat she'd get this week, and it was gone. Just then, a chocolate bar appeared in front of her. "Come on," Ryan said, "have some of this. I'll get you another one."

Lara stood up and began to make her way to the witness stand. Jun grabbed her hand.

"Lara, don't-" His eyes met hers and he froze. Lara serenely extracted her hand away from him and continued.

She was nine. Her hands were blistered and bruised. It was the first time she held a gun, and she was already made to practice for hours. A tube of aloe vera gel was thrown in front of her. "Crybaby," Ryan said with a frown, "I got this for you. Might help with those ugly hands of yours."

A strong gust of wind blew across the room; papers, hats and coats circled around the room. Lara walked in the middle of this, unfazed.

Arthur also ran over to her, as if wanting to say something. But when Lara turned to face him, he immediately backed away.

She was eleven. She was pushed onto the ground. Ryan had stomped into her training session for no reason, his face flushed and he stunk like alcohol. He kicked her gun away and screamed like a madman. "Stop training, you fucking idiot! Stop trying to be an Operative!" She bawled from the shock and bolted out of the training room.

She ambled towards Ryan. The brown-haired man was frowning and shaking his head. Was he telling her to leave? It didn't matter. She walked past the rows of benches, walked past the thousands of appalled faces, walked past the police officers who stood aghast and unmoving, and walked past the judge.

She was fourteen. Ryan was passed out on the floor, drunk. Lara rolled her eyes and reached for him. What an idiot, he needs to stop going out to the bars. But when she held him up, he grabbed onto her shoulders, as if clinging onto dear life. "Lara, I'm so sorry," he whispered, "it's all my fault, it's all my fault, all my fault..."

Ryan was staring at her, his expression unreadable. She grabbed the handcuffs on his hands, and with an effortless pinch, she shattered it into pieces. The metal fragments rained down onto the floor; the light, tinkling sound juxtaposed the deafening, gusting winds that were becoming stronger and stronger by the second.

"Let's go," she said. Her voice was so unfamiliar that it scared even herself, but she remained surprisingly calm about it. "Let's get out of here."

Ryan sighed. Then, he gave Lara a hard smack on her head.

The winds stopped. The items that were swept away fell onto the ground with a swish. Lara staggered from the impact, her hand on her throbbing temple. She blinked as her mind gradually cleared.

"Learn how to control your Gift, baby Lara," Ryan said with a low voice.

"B- But Ryan, we have to redo this trial!" Lara shrieked. Her normal, wimpy voice was back. "You can't die!"

"I told you, I'm going to atone for my sins." Ryan patted Lara's head. "But you're in good hands now. I'm happy for you."

"No!" Lara yelled. "You're not leaving me! I'm not letting anybody leave me anymore!" She grabbed Ryan's hands as tightly as she could. "My parents are dead, Madam has been lying to me my whole life, Arianna is not here, please, Ryan, I only have you. Please."

"Don't be such a baby." Ryan snorted. "You stay alive and happy, okay? Don't ever be sad about a guy like me."

And then, with a forceful thrust in the chest, Ryan pushed Lara away. She stumbled backwards and fell on her butt. Her teary eyes watched helplessly as Ryan strolled towards the police officers behind him.

"Hey, come on, my handcuffs are gone, you gonna give me another one, or what?"

***

6

---

fifteen years ago —

Ryan leaned against the bed rail and peered down. Sleeping soundly in a fetal position was a two-year-old girl; her drool stained her pillow, and her locks of hair fluttered whenever she breathed out. He poked at his sister's pudgy, rosy cheeks. Her nose twitched as she moaned in protest.

Delighted, he couldn't help but chuckle. He then proceeded to poke at her cheeks over and over again, as she squirmed in discomfort.

"You're having a lot of fun teasing Lara, huh."

Ryan spun around. When he saw the auburn-haired woman standing by the wooden door, he sighed in relief. "Oh, hey, Aunt Ari," he said, silently thanking the lords that it wasn't his mother. Even though Arianna was quite intimidating, at least she wouldn't berate him for disturbing Lara. "Yeah, it's really funny when she's annoyed."

Arianna narrowed her eyes sullenly. She looked very much like his father, with the same reddish brown hair, slightly upturned nose and bright blue eyes, but somehow, every single feature was a lot harsher and colder. It was as if she was forever displeased with her life. Ryan always wondered what was it that made her so different from his father; they grew up together, yet their personalities were a world apart.

"I hope you treasure these moments then," she said bitterly. "You won't be happy with her very soon."

"Why?" Ryan frowned. He had to stop himself from saying, "Was she going to turn into a grumpy butt like you or something?" But he knew that if he ever said that, his mother would definitely spank the hell out of him.

Arianna rolled her eyes. "Has your father not told you? He chose her as the next bearer of Hope."

"Oh yeah, I knew that already."

"And you're okay with that?" Arianna asked, glancing at Ryan in slight disbelief.

"Well yeah, Dad told me she's born under this special star and so the Gift will be the strongest for her, so she should get it instead of me." Ryan shrugged. All his life, his parents were always making decisions based on how they would best benefit the war against the First Lady Elena: the living embodiment of terror and cruelty. Lara was apparently destined to become Elena's most formidable enemy, although Ryan was pretty sure his father was going to defeat Elena anyway.

"Plus, I don't really care for it," he continued. "Why would I need a Gift for?"

Arianna was silent for a while. Then, she muttered under her breath, "That's what you'll think for now." She turned around sharply. "Your father is preparing to leave for a mission soon, by the way, you should go see him before he leaves."

"Oh, okay." Ryan felt his heart sink. He was used to his parents leaving frequently, but it was still hard not to feel a little disappointed at the news. "Are you going to go too?"

His aunt's back stiffened. "Yes and no," she said without even turning around. She promptly left the tent, slamming the makeshift door shut.

Ryan was utterly perplexed. What did she mean by that? Was she going, or not? His aunt had always been unusually cryptic, for some reason. He decided to shift his attention back to Lara.

The tiny brunette was fully awake by now, her round, brown eyes staring at Ryan eagerly.

"Yan-Yan!" she squealed.

Ryan squealed internally as well. He really wanted to reach out and squeeze her cheeks, but the last time he did that, Lara cried for hours (and his flogged butt hurt for days). Instead, he lightly prodded her nose. "I guess it's just going to be me and you for the next few days, or however long this mission is going to be."

Lara obviously didn't understand a word he said. She continued chanting Ryan's name while giggling hysterically.

"I see you had a really good nap, huh?" Ryan grinned. "Anyway, I'm going to go find Mom and Dad now, but I'll come back soon. Stay here, okay?"

He made his way out of the tent, his feet light and his mood cheerful. The temporary village they were living in was spotted with large makeshift barracks that were designed to match their colors to the surrounding. As he hopped along the gravel road, he passed by a bunch of playsets that he had built himself: some trapeze bars, tire swings, and a slide twice his own height. His mother had forbidden him from bringing Lara to these playsets, but one day, though, once she's bigger, he promised to himself to let her try them.

Ryan's parents moved around a lot, and thus he had grown up living in temporary villages like this. According to his parents, they were trying to gather allies or something, although Ryan never really understood much of it. All he knew was that it was extremely difficult to make friends his age; everytime he attempted to befriend someone, he would have to leave for a new city or realm after a few months. Luckily, he had Lara now, and life wasn't as boring as it had been before.

He entered one of the biggest tents in the village. Surprisingly, it was filled with people, as if the entire town had congregated in there. The adults were all chatting and murmuring to one another solemnly. A large, round table sat in the middle; maps, papers and other unknown items sprawled across it messily.

Ryan scanned the room and found his parents huddled in a corner with their friends, Soo-Rin and Ren. He rushed over to them, shouting jubilantly, "Mom! Dad!"

Min-Ju squatted down and welcomed Ryan as he jumped into her arms. As they embraced, her long brown hair enveloped his body like a warm, fluffy blanket. He closed his eyes and breathed in the familiar lavender scent.

"Ryan, I told you not to come in here," Marco chided gently, his arms crossed.

Ryan lifted his head and pouted at his father. "But Aunt Ari told me you're leaving!"

Min-Ju smiled and patted his head. "Yes, we will be leaving tonight, but not to worry, we will be back tomorrow by the latest. You take care of Lara while we're gone, okay?"

Ryan nodded. "Dinner at six, bedtime by nine," he recited monotonously.

"And that goes for you too," his mother reminded him.

"What! No! I don't want to sleep that early."

Min-Ju raised an index finger. "Ryan." Her tone was tender but stern. "If I check the screen time in your console and find out you've been up past nine, I will take it away for a month."

Ryan had to fight back his eyerolls. His mother was not someone he could argue with. "Fine..." he mumbled.

The two other adults standing by the side laughed heartily.

"Oh, I envy you so much, Min-Ju," Soo-Rin said. "If only we knew earlier how good of a babysitter Ryan is, we would've totally brought Jun over with us too!" Soo-Rin was Min-Ju's childhood friend, and Ryan liked her and her husband quite a bit. He wasn't a fan of Jun though; that kid was annoying and cried too much, so Ryan was secretly glad that he didn't need to deal with him.

"Yes, our Ryan here is the best big brother in the world, aren't you?" Min-Ju crooned, her eyes shimmering with pride. Ryan beamed at the praise.

Marco crouched down as well. "Ryan, we need you to take really good care of your sister while we're gone, okay? Remember, she's very important, she's-"

"I know, I know." Ryan heaved an exasperated sigh. His father had nagged him about this so many times, he really didn't need to hear it again. "She's born under the star of Nadia, she's the next bearer of Elissa's First Gift, the next Hope, right?"

Marco nodded wistfully. "I just need you to know the reason why I chose her and not you." A storm cloud of regret seemed to have invaded his sky blue eyes. "I don't want you to be upset like-"

Min-Ju placed a hand on Marco's shoulder. "Ryan understands. He's a good boy," she said with a reassuring smile. "We also finally got Arianna to be in on the plan, didn't we? We've always needed someone as skilled as her."

Marco squeezed her hand as they exchanged a knowing look with each other.

"So Aunt Ari is going after all," Ryan mused. "Is everyone else going too?"

"Yes, this is the raid that we've been planning for months, so everyone is going." Min-Ju gestured at her friends. "Except for Soo-Rin and Ren here, who are going to stay behind to protect you two children. We don't feel safe leaving you two completely alone."

"Oh." Ryan realized the severity of this mission. This must be the ultimate, secret raid of the First Lady's headquarters on Earth that his parents had been preparing for for the longest time. He shuddered a little at that thought. "Erm, good luck, Mom, I hope it goes well."

"Thank you, Ryan, and don't worry, it will." Min-Ju placed her hand on her son's cheeks and gave it a light pinch. "Okay, we need to get back to preparing now. Go back to Lara, alright?"

"Okay," Ryan said before hurriedly leaving the tent. Excited to play with Lara, he sprinted back home as fast as he could, only to burst into his home and find his baby sister fast asleep on her bed again. He groaned. She was so full of energy just moments ago!

He wanted to shake Lara awake, but quickly decided against it. Instead, he slumped onto the couch next to her and started up his gaming console. For the next few hours, he focused on reaching the next level of his RPG.

The alarm rang exactly at six in the evening, forcibly tearing Ryan away from his game. He let out a string of curses that would've earned him a good whipping —Argh! He was so close to beating that last boss!— and looked around the tent. His sister was still lying on her bed; the golden rays of the sun peeked through the canvas screen, causing her to glow like an angel.

He rubbed his eyes and took a peep of the village outside. The whole place was empty, except for Soo-Rin and Ren sitting on a bench a few hundred feet down. They seemed to be murmuring to each other, their heads low and their hands clasped together. Everyone else must have already left for the mission.

Ryan raised his hand for a stretch and proceeded to prepare for dinner. He first grabbed a small bottle of milk from the fridge and let it sit inside a warm water bath. While waiting, he cut up some vegetables and whipped up some eggs.

At this point, Lara finally woke up from the noise and was bouncing up and down on the bed. Ryan took the heated milk bottle and gave it to her; she seized it with fervor and began to chug on it.

Suddenly, Ryan's phone, placed precariously on the kitchen countertop, began to buzz. Who would be calling him at a time like this?

Oh, it was Min-Ju, video-calling him. Huh. Weird.

He picked up his phone and accepted the call. And then almost dropped his phone.

His mother was on the other end of the call, bleeding and gasping for air. Her face, her hair, her neck... all of her that Ryan could see on the phone screen, was soaked in blood. Panting heavily, she pushed out a weak smile when she saw Ryan's face —even her teeth were stained with blood.

"Ryan," Min-Ju whispered. Her voice was frail and hoarse. "Oh, thank the heavens, Ryan..."

"Mom!" Ryan screamed. "What happened?"

"It's okay, Ryan, everything is okay. Mommy loves you, okay? Stay with Soo-Rin and Ren, and keep Lara safe, okay? Oh, Lara... Can I please see Lara one last time, Ryan?"

Ryan, however, remained frozen in shock. His hands were trembling, barely holding onto his phone, but every other part of his body was hardened in place, unable to move.

"Ryan? Can I please see her? Can I see Lara?"

What the hell, what the hell, what in the hell... Why was his mother bleeding like that, and why was she begging to see Lara, as if it was her last chance of seeing her ever? Ryan's mind was crumbling into pieces; as his mother continued begging and pleading with her dying breath, he could only stand there, silent, unmoving, utterly stupefied.

Something tugged on his pants. He glanced down; his neck was stiff and sweaty. It was Lara. The little girl had gotten off her bed and was staring at him cheerily. "Yan-Yan!" she exclaimed.

Min-Ju must have heard that, because she became even more deranged. "Lara!!!" She used every ounce of her energy to cry out. "Lara, my baby daughter! Ryan, please! Please, let me see Lara one last time, please? Mommy loves you and Lara very much, okay? I want to see her one last time..."

Ryan raised his shaky fingers, and tried to flip the camera over, but he couldn't press anything. No, his tears had blurred his vision so much that he couldn't even see his mother anymore. His heart was also beating so fast he could no longer hear his mother's desperate sobs, and his body had become so numb that he couldn't feel Lara pulling on his leg.

No, no... He can't be watching his mother die on his phone... That's not right... That's not how the mission should've gone... That's not how any of this should've ended...

"Hang in there, Mom!" Ryan shouted so loudly and abruptly that Lara fell backwards, startled. "I'll- I'll come get you!"

He looked around frantically. What can he do? How can he find her? What should he do? His head was simultaneously empty and filled with thoughts at the same time; like a blank piece of paper that Lara had drawn illegibly on. Mom was dying, she was in another realm, she was dying, and there was nothing he could do.

A helpless whimper escaped his throat. He wanted nothing more than to be able to teleport right next to his mother and save her. How he wished he had a Gift right now, how he wished that his father had granted him with the Gift of Hope, how he wished he could go and help them right now...

All of the sudden, the entire world swirled into dark shadows. When the blackness cleared, Ryan found himself in an unfamiliar environment. It was some kind of a building, with curved ceilings and shiny white walls.

And there she was —his mother, flat on the ground, her long hair sprawled all over. A trail of blood extended from behind her, indicating a clear path from where she was crawling from.

"Mom!" Ryan cried as he ran towards the injured woman.

Min-Ju raised her head, fear washed over her blood-drenched face. "Ryan, what are you- how are you..."

"I- I don't know!" Ryan stammered. "But I'm here now, Mom! I'm going to save you!" He tried to lift her mother up, but she groaned in pain and pushed him away.

"N- No... You're not supposed to get the Gift, it's your sister..."

"I know, but I don't know how... I don't know how but I got a Gift, Mom, I- I teleported here, somehow..." Ryan wiped his tears off; his face was now smeared with his own mother's blood. "Let me bring you home, Mom, let me save you..."

"No, no, no..." Min-Ju sobbed. "Elissa's Gift, the Gift of Hope... It's Lara, it's supposed to be Lara, not you... She's supposed to be the new Hope, she could end this, she could end Elena's reign-"

She started coughing vigorously. As Ryan reached out to her again, she held onto his arm and sobbed hysterically into his sleeve.

Ryan had cried into his mother's arms like this so many times in his life, but never would he ever imagine that he would one day see her weep like a child too. "Mom, I'm sorry... I'm so, so sorry... I- I didn't mean to, I don't know what happened... I really don't..."

Then, she stopped moving.

"Mom?" Ryan whispered. His mother had slumped onto his arms, motionless and cold.

"Mom, don't scare me like this..." He shook her body. She still did not move.

Finally, Ryan pushed her body over. His mother's eyes and mouth remained wide open. Her dark brown eyes still had a beautiful sheen from the leftover tears, but the usual spark of joy was completely gone. Red river streamed down from the top of her head; the mixture of blood, sweat and tears swirled around her lifeless face.

She was dead.

The dread that Ryan had been holding inside of him burst. He buried his head into Min-Ju's hair, and let out a wail. The hair tickled his face, muffling his uncontrollable cries; it was still so soft and so warm, reminding him of her bear hug, her kind smile, her gentle voice. Underneath the repugnant smell of iron, the distinct lavender shampoo still permeated. The more he breathed in, the more he wanted to scream out in anguish. The more his body buckled into his mother's corpse, the more he wanted to turn back time, to stop his parents from going on this mission, to bring his mother back alive...

Please... I just want Mom back...

After what seemed like forever, Ryan lifted his head. Despite his blurred vision, he noticed a dagger a few feet away from them. A thought struck him. Slowly, he walked over to the knife and picked it up. It was soaked in blood, but at this point, what wasn't?

He followed the trail of blood, trudging along the corridor; the glossy, metallic walls made the entire building seem paper white. For some reason, he got the coveted Gift of Untrodden Hope. Not Lara, the person destined to get it, but him. And for some reason, with this all-powerful First Gift that allows the bearer to develop any Gift they want, he developed a Gift of teleportation. Not super strength like his father, no, and not clairvoyance like his grandmother either —it was teleportation. Fucking teleportation.

But that was okay. He was going to use this Gift to help his parents end this war. He was going to kill Elena. He was going to avenge his mother.

The blood trail made a turn. He carefully peeked around the corner, and had to cover his mouth to stop a gasp.

In the middle of a spacious hall hung a metal chain. A man's legs were shackled to the chain, while the rest of his body dangled upside-down. His ripped clothes, broken limbs, and auburn hair were splattered with blood; as he swayed a little in the air, trickles of blood dripped down on the floor, as though they were painting an abstract, pointillism art on a pure, white canvas.

Ryan felt his stomach churn —the man was his father! No, no, focus, Ryan! Using all of his willpower, he forced himself to swallow back his vomit and concentrated on the other two people in the room.

Standing in front of his father was a tall woman in a green, elegant gown. Her long platinum blonde hair was embellished with a shiny tiara; a hefty emerald glittered under the light, its beauty was a stark contrast to the twisted, cruel smile she was wearing.

And next to that strange woman, to Ryan's surprise, was Arianna. Miniature gusts of air and dirt spun around her cupped hands; her long auburn hair fluttered about from the wind. Wait, did she get a Gift as well? And a really cool one at that, too. How? Why was everyone who was not supposed to have a Gift getting one today?

But that didn't matter at all. Right now, his focus was on the green dress lady. She must be Elena, the First Lady of Earth, the cursed traitor, the reign of terror. The person who was responsible for all of this.

He was going to kill Elena. He was going to avenge his parents.

He tightened his grip on the dagger and closed his eyes.

When he opened his eyes again, he was right next to Elena. Immediately, he raised his hand and got ready to stab her. Before the knife could even reach her, however, an icy voice sent a shiver down his spine.

"Stop."

An invisible force crushed down on Ryan on all sides; his body froze, his lungs squeezed and deflated, his grip loosened. He watched helplessly as the dagger slipped out of his hand and dropped onto the floor, while Elena turned around calmly.

"Oh hello, little one, who are you?" she said, her sickly sweet voice was both pleasant and horrifying.

Oh shit.

Ryan's heart leapt up to his throat, as he knew that he made a terrible, terrible mistake. He had forgotten about Elena's Gift, the Gift of Faith, the most frightening Gift of them all. Of all things to forget, how could he ever forget about that?

He needed to get out of here, now.

And so, he did what he thought was the next best thing: he closed his eyes and willed himself to teleport.

The disgusting, gory scene around him engulfed in darkness, and soon, he was back in the familiar homely tent. Lara was playing with her doll, an empty milk bottle was rolling around the kitchen floor, a plate of chopped vegetables sat on the countertop. He sighed in relief.

But that relief was short-lived.

"My oh my, what is this place?"

Ryan felt as though he was punched in the gut. He was still unable to move, but he didn't need to turn his head to know who it was. It appeared that Elena's hand was on his shoulder all this time, and he never even realized.

And he had brought Elena home. To Lara.

***

7

"Hello!" the little girl squealed, looking up at the First Lady with a pair of bright, eager eyes. "Hello, hello!"

Ryan watched helplessly as Elena squatted down and patted his younger sister's head. His limbs were still locked in that same awkward position from when he tried to stab Elena. The windpipe in his throat was semi-blocked too, and his head was spinning from a lack of oxygen; he couldn't even call out to Lara, tell her to stay away from Elena, stay away from the person responsible for their parents' death, stay away from that wicked, cruel, insane, horrifying monster...

"Hello there, are you Marco's special little daughter?" Elena crooned as she stretched out her hands. Lara readily plopped into her arms, squirming and giggling while Elena tickled her neck.

"I can't believe I got to meet you," the blonde woman continued. "I've heard so much about you, you know? The special little daughter born under the star of Nadia. Aren't you supposed to receive Elissa's Gift, and then become the strongest person in the world, surpassing even me? But you didn't end up actually getting the Gift, did you?"

She turned her attention to Ryan, and her smile twisted. "Instead, you got the Gift, and you're really, really weak. Well, lucky me, I guess." She stood up and sauntered towards the young boy, her expression filled with mirth and condescension. "And I must thank you for bringing me to Marco's secret home base, I really appreciate it. I will be sure to end this traitorous realm completely."

Ryan's heart sank, as if it had turned into stone and plunged into a bottomless abyss. What had he done? Beyond this village, the realm was inhabited by people who had fled Elena's rule, including his parents' friends, families and allies. And now, he had not only revealed the location to Elena, but had also brought her, unscathed and unguarded, past all the defenses and battlers of the realm.

Worst of all, he had brought her to Lara, the one person he was tasked to protect.

Elena couldn't stop smiling at Ryan's crestfallen face as she pressed her palms against his head. Instantly, his vision was blurred by sparkles of light and his head began to spin. He let out a soft sob before collapsing face down on the ground, tired and drained.

"Yan-Yan?" Lara tilted her head. She quickly ignored her confusion, however, when Elena handed her her doll back while caressing her.

"Don't worry, my dear, he's okay, I just took away his Gift," Elena reassured the young brunette. "Or tried to, at least, I can't seem to take away his Gift completely." She flipped the groaning boy over with her foot. "But that's okay, I've weakened you so much that you're essentially useless now. So much for getting a Gift, huh?"

She casted one last smirk at Ryan before stepping over his slumped torso; her cold, silky gown brushed against his pale, sweaty skin, sending shivers down his spine. "Now, let's take a look at this realm, shall we?" she announced as she waltzed out of the tent.

Ryan tried to get up, but whatever Elena had done to him, it must have sapped away all of his energy. Right now, he was finding it difficult to even keep his eyelids open. But he knew he had to somehow get up and leave; the crazy bitch was gone so this was the perfect time to escape.

Laboriously, he rolled himself over, such that he was facing his sister. She was now back to playing with her doll, humming blissfully, not a care in the world. "Lara..." he called out with a weak, hoarse voice. "Come here, Lara, let's get out of here..."

Bang! Bang!

Ryan jolted in shock from the sudden gunshots. Dread welled up inside his heart —was that Soo-Rin and Ren? Lara also looked around the tent, frowning and curious, but relatively unfazed. Before he could attempt to call Lara over again, Elena came back.

"Interesting, so Bernu was the home base they chose. I wasn't informed of that, nor was I expecting that." Elena wiped her hands on her gown, her nose scrunched up slightly in disgust. "Though, maybe I should've guessed from the wife he picked."

A whimper escaped Ryan's dry throat. It was too late, everything was too late; everyone in his life had died, and he couldn't even protect Lara now. The toddler, on the other hand, perked up at the sight of the First Lady, and bounced over to her excitedly.

Elena chuckled and rubbed Lara's soft, brown hair. "Aw, it seems you've taken a liking to me, how ironic." She hoisted the delighted girl up and walked over to Ryan. "Alright, do your job, child, I'm bored of this place."

With a forceful grab, she snatched Ryan up by the arms, ignoring his cries of agony. "Take me back."

Ryan's entire body was aching, and he had never felt more exhausted in his life. But under Elena's command, he had no choice but to use his newly blessed Gift again. He closed his eyes, and teleported all three of them back to Earth.

When the darkness cleared, he crumpled on the ground like a ragdoll. Blood, water, bile, gastric acid, every possible fluid from within Ryan, gushed out from him like a sputtering engine of a busted car. He didn't have the energy to moan in pain; he didn't even have the energy to cough the liquids out of his mouth.

Somewhere in front of him laid a body; even with sweat and tears obscuring his vision, he was still able to recognize Marco's bloodied corpse. Was he also going to die right next to his father? At that moment, he wasn't sure if the stream of liquid flowing down his face was his tears, sweat, or the disgusting mixture of fluid he had just puked out.

Arianna was kneeling next to Marco's body, her face hung low and her fists clenched. When she saw the three of them appearing out of thin air, she blanched.

"M- Madam," she stuttered while scrambling to stand up, "you found Lara, the next bearer."

Elena laughed. "Not really. As it turns out, she's not the next bearer, this guy is."

"What? Ryan is?" Arianna asked incredulously. "But- But Lara was supposed to be-"

"Who knows? Maybe Marco made a mistake, as he did when he chose to marry a Bernuian woman." The First Lady shrugged. "But that's good for us. This boy is weak, and I've turned him into someone who can only teleport once before passing out. I mean, look at him now." She casually gave Ryan a kick in his stomach. Ryan retched even more.

Elena proceeded to smoothe Lara's hair; the energetic girl had been playing with the tiara on her head, distracted and oblivious of her surroundings. "And this girl, this famous Lara Carland, the supposed next bearer of Hope, she's just a Gift-less baby. So what if she's destined to be powerful, there's absolutely nothing she can do right now."

Arianna stared at Ryan, then at Lara. "Madam," she probed warily, "what are you planning to do with them..."

"Kill them, of course."

"But Madam, they're- they're just children..."

Elena raised her eyebrows. "Are you questioning my decisions? Now that I've given you the Gift you've longed for, are you becoming bold?"

The redhead flushed and shook her head vigorously. "No, I'm... I'm not. I'm very grateful for everything you've done, Madam."

Elena's piercing gaze did not leave Arianna, who had suddenly become very interested in the blood-stained floors. Then, her mouth slowly curled up. "You know what, I have a better idea."

She lifted Lara high up in the air, who giggled and squealed in joy. "Isn't she destined to become the most formidable person on Earth? Well, I'm going to let her live up to her destiny, but instead, she'll be on my side. I'm going to have her end all the Turned Realms. Imagine, they all thought that she will become their saviour, but this saviour of theirs will actually be their downfall." She let out a laugh that made Ryan's skin crawl, but managed to keep Lara charmed. "I wonder how Elissa would feel, too, having her descendant work for me. After all, I'm this vile and horrendous person she never wished to have as a sister, right?"

Elena cradled Lara once more; her alluring, sweet voice was increasingly tainted with bitterness and spite. "And I'll be sure to give you the Gift that betrayed and killed your parents, too," she added with a whisper. "You're going to become the antithesis of what you're supposed to be. It's going to be so delightful."

Ryan finally managed to summon one last ounce of strength in him. "No..." he gasped. "Lara... Don't take her..."

"Why?" Elena dropped Lara onto a flustered Arianna, and approached the half-conscious boy. "What are you going to do about it?"

Ryan could only heave out a throaty breath as a reply. This earned a maniacal chortle from Elena.

"I can't believe my luck! The new bearer of Hope is so weak, even weaker than Marco! I was right all along; if you pass down your Gift, it'll just become weaker. Elissa really should've listened to me and never done that, but I guess that's what she gets for falling in love with a human man."

Elena pinched Ryan's cheeks together with one hand, and pulled him towards her.

"Ah, I'm so tempted to just kill you and end this stupid Hope Gift once and for all. And then, I'll be the only person who possesses the First Gifts," she murmured as she relished in the obvious pain that he was in. "But I'm not going to let you be with your parents so easily. I also want you to work for me; it's going to be so hilarious watching you try to complete missions with a weak Gift like yours. And I also want you to watch your sister grow up, watch her despise you, watch her become a monster, become the ultimate reign of terror against your own people."

Ryan wanted to cry, but he ended up coughing out even more blood. The older woman shoved him back down, and he fell onto the ground, wheezing and choking.

Arianna was holding onto Lara tightly, humming a soft lullaby into her ear. She had always hated children, and never wanted anything to do with Ryan or Lara, but right now, she was handling the toddler with such care and affection, as if she had somehow appointed herself the new mother.

When Elena turned to Arianna, the auburn-haired woman paled.

"So, their home base was actually in Bernu." The First Lady's calm, low voice was coated with a cold, stinging layer of ice. "You told me it was in Honnu."

Arianna hid her trembling hand by caressing Lara's hair. "I'm sorry, Madam... I must have gotten the wrong information."

"Did you, now?" Elena did not sound as though she believed her. "Come with me, then. Finish what you started." With that, she strode away from the hall.

Arianna gulped, a mix of emotions flashed through her face. Then, she casted one last look at Ryan before following the blonde woman, Lara in her hands.

The place was now empty, except for two disheveled bodies. Ryan sprawled on the floor, still unmoving, still panting, still hacking out blood occasionally. His eyes landed on his father's corpse, and he closed them shut.

So much for being the best big brother in the world. He had taken the Gift that was meant for Lara, and ruined it with his incompetence; he had brought the enemy to their secret home base, and betrayed the entire realm; worst of all, he had given Lara straight to the enemy, and destroyed her destiny.

This was all his fault... All his fault...

So much for being the best big brother in the world.

Mom, Dad, I'm so sorry.

— two days ago —

Ryan stared up at the white ceiling of the sick bay. His hands were burning like crazy, and his arms were aching like hell, but whatever.

At least he made it out of the training room; he'd honestly thought he was going to spend the rest of his life there. The pain was also nothing compared to the stuff he had to endure for the past fifteen years.

Physical pain, in general, was nothing to him. It was too easy to fix; the doctors here would have no issues treating his injuries, just for him to get back here a few weeks later or so. Get injured, get treated, get injured, get treated — it was a never ending cycle for fifteen years.

Physical pain was nothing to him, but the pain that's eating him up inside him, though, now that was something. The doctors had given him some pills to take that numbed the pain, but it never went away, not like these physical injuries.

Someone new was checking into the sick bay, and the voice was really familiar. Ryan lifted his head to see, rolled his eyes and laid back down on the bed.

Several nurses rushed over to help the frail newcomer. Her ghostly pale complexion was covered in cold sweat and she looked like she could barely stand. As she settled onto the bed next to Ryan, one doctor helped her set up an IV fluid drip, while the other nurses worked on getting her vitals.

When the doctor and nurses left, Ryan peered at the redhead in contempt. "What are you? Losing your Gift?" he said with a snort.

Arianna did not reply. Well, Ryan wasn't really expecting a reply anyway. They had not been on talking terms for fifteen years now, exchanging a few words only in Lara's presence.

Ryan continued his staring contest with the ceiling. After what seemed like forever, he finally decided to break the silence.

"So, was it worth it?" he asked quietly. "Was all of this worth it for a Gift?"

The woman turned her back towards Ryan. He rolled his eyes again. How Lara was able to stand being around this gloomy little butt like her, he could never understand. Then again, she had a totally different personality in front of Lara. Two-faced bitch.

"You don't know how it feels."

Ryan frowned, slightly taken aback that Arianna actually said something to him. "What?"

Arianna's back was still facing Ryan; her long, auburn hair draped over the bed like a bunch of wilting flowers. "You don't know how it feels like, always living in the shadows of a sibling who got every-thing," she repeated bitterly.

Ryan stared at the middle-aged woman for a long time, and then burst into hysterical laughter. He covered his eyes with an arm, and laughed so loud that the nurses were giving him the stink eye. Then, he rolled over in his bed, and laughed until tears came —tears that had been dried and used up ever since that day, tears that were appearing for the first time in fifteen years.

"No, I don't know how it feels like," he said after he calmed down, "but you know what? I really wished I did."

He hopped off his bed and stretched his upper body. "A'ight, I'm gonna go get a drink. I can't stand being around you any longer."

As he walked by her bed to leave, he casted one last cheeky grin at her. "Aunt Ari."

— present —

He was leaning against the cold, grimy wall, his head hung low. The disheveled brown hair was stuck to his sweaty face, further blinding his already poor vision. Blood from his mouth trickled on the chains around his arms, the endless drips sounded like the ticking of the clock. Every part of his body was screaming in pain, but he was far too exhausted and famished to notice. How long ago was it since he had last eaten, or drank?

Ah, Nightlaza Bar. That was the last place he'd gotten something to eat. Wow, so the last meal of his life was going to be trash bar food, huh? What a life.

The metal door slammed open.

"You have fifteen minutes," a voice boomed. "Any other requests?"

It took Ryan all his strength and willpower just to lift his head and look at the burly prison guard. "You sent that message?" he croaked. He was surprised his voice still worked.

"Yeah." The prison guard frowned. "That short message is all you want to send?" Despite his jaded, let's-get-this-over-with tone, the guard was still visibly perplexed by Ryan's unusual lack of emotion over his impending death. It was as if Ryan was too comfortable with the idea of death.

He really was, though. Honestly, he had been waiting for this day for fifteen years. Every other week, he had scaled up the headquarters and sat on the roof, a place no one was technically allowed to go. Then, he would just stare down from the top of the ten-storey high building, contemplating. Maybe it'd be easier if he jumped, maybe it'd be less painful if he ended this, maybe he could see his parents again if he did this... And he'd suddenly think about Lara; the thought of Lara being left alone with Arianna and Elena killed him on the inside even more. He couldn't leave her, not after what he had done to her.

But now? Now, everything was good. Everything was back to normal. His Gift really had been just a mistake, a fluke. It turned out that he didn't steal the Gift of Hope from Lara; she was still the next bearer, she still had the ability to counter Elena's Gift, just as his parents had predicted. Not only that, she was given Arianna's Gift. Of all Gifts, she got Arianna's.

Now, she was so powerful, and so much stronger than Elena and her strongest Operative. Yet, she was still the same, kind-hearted little girl: the girl who cried for days after Ryan accidentally killed her pet fish; the girl who absolutely abhorred him but still took care of him every time he came back home drunk; the girl who was taught to hate the Turned Realms but could not bear to even kill one Karzian boy. All these years with Arianna and Elena didn't seem to have tainted her heart at all.

He still couldn't believe that she actually went against her beliefs, and risked it all just to not kill one person. Ryan could not help but chuckle. What did this say about him, then? He had had zero qualms eradicating millions of people, just to hold on a little longer.

But it's okay, everything was good now. He had brought Lara back, she was being taken care of by the Karzians, she was even hanging out with Jun —didn't they used to play together a lot? This was good. All was good now. He can rest. Permanently.

Oh wait. Wasn't it Lara's birthday two days ago?

He silently cursed at himself. He was meant to buy her a present that day but he got sidetracked by that trash bar. But well, saving Lara from Elena's headquarters should be a good enough birthday present? Right?

Ah, I'm the worst brother.

"One more thing," he said, his voice soft and hoarse, "could you give my phone to Lara?" That was probably the only item of value that he owned. She already had one, but his model was the newer, better one, so maybe she might like it.

"Yeah, sure." The guard gestured impatiently towards the door. "If there's nothing else, let's go then."

Ryan heaved himself off the ground. He staggered a little, as his metal chains scraped against his bruised limbs. "Ah, right." He suddenly remembered something. "Could you also help me delete all the dick pics from my phone before you give it to her or something?"

"Hell no."

"Figured." Ryan shrugged. "Eh whatever, she's eighteen already. Lead the way, my good guy."

The guard marched out of the room, and Ryan tried his best to trail behind. Despite being a prison, the rugged concrete walls and yellow tint of the light made the place feel so much warmer than that hellhole he had lived in. He smiled.

Mom, Dad, I can't wait to see you again.

***

8

Outside the hotel, the Karzian city nightlife was bustling and lively. Chatters and laughters filled the air, embellished with the sporadic tinkling sounds of cutlery from the restaurants. The moon hung bright on the night sky, but its light was drowned out by the even brighter city lights on the ground.

The inside of the hotel room, however, was eerily dark and quiet; it was as if all the sounds and lights from the streets were sucked into a vacuum the moment they travelled through the hotel window. Lara was lying on her bed, face buried into her tear-soaked pillow. The cheer and happiness of the streets seemed to be mocking her, making her curl up even more under the blanket.

Today was the day. Ryan was going to die today.

Occasionally, she could hear murmurs of the sentencing outside. The Operative of Elena. The infamous traitor of the Bernuian raid fifteen years ago. The murderer responsible for Elena's continued reign of terror. The more she heard, the more she pressed her head into her pillow. Shut up, shut up, shut up!

Why did he let himself get sentenced to death just like that? Why did he look like he was so ready to leave? Why would he do that? Why would he leave her like that? She knew they had fought all the time and that they had always been mean to each other... but they still grew up together. Why would he just leave her alone like that? Why, why, why?

Arianna.

Lara's heart clenched as she thought of her auburn-haired friend. How she wished she could cry into Arianna's arms and listen to her calm, soothing voice. She wanted nothing more than to go back home, back to her simpler life, before she received a Gift, before her eighteenth birthday, before this all went downhill. But right now, home had never felt more unfamiliar and frightening.

There was a knock on the door. It was probably Jun.

"Come in," she croaked, her voice muffled by the pillow.

The sudden sting on her eyeballs told her that the lights were turned on. She felt Jun sit down next to her on the bed, placing something on the bedside table. Slowly, she lifted her head to greet her visitor.

"I got you a smoothie," Jun mumbled, his face averted slightly. "Since you don't seem to be eating normal foods, I thought maybe you'd like liquid food instead."

Lara nodded appreciatively. Jun and Arthur had been checking up on her for the past few hours, but she had been too distraught to be comforted. Feeling apologetic, she forced a smile and took a sip of the smoothie. Her tongue had lost the ability to taste anything, while her throat was clogged, but she managed to push a few gulps down —just enough to bring a bit of relief to Jun.

The Bernuian boy glanced at Lara. "Anyway, he, erm..." He paused, taking out a phone from his pocket. "He left this for you."

Lara blinked. Ryan... actually left her something? Her trembling hands reached out for the device. The moment it touched her skin, the rectangular block shrunk in size and molded its shape to fit her palms. Then, the phone unlocked by itself, adjusting its brightness to the exact level of intensity her eyes needed.

This was the latest model Android Axis 8.21. She still remembered how the tall man had gloated about this phone when he had first gotten it. A lump grew inside her throat, but she swallowed back her tears.

"Why did he leave you his phone?" Jun asked, shifting closer to Lara for a peek at the device. "Did he leave some kind of message in there or something?"

"I... I don't know..." Lara admitted. She never knew what was going on inside that guy's head. Even to his last days, he still insisted on being as annoyingly mysterious as ever, it seemed.

She swiped around the phone. There were a lot of different maps and encyclopedia-like apps that she was unfamiliar with. The only app she knew was the photos app, and so she decided to select it.

Instantly, the two teenagers screamed out in terror.

"Ew!" Lara shrieked as her grip on the phone loosened. Thankfully, the device remained glued to her palm.

"Oh my God, what is wrong with him?" Jun cried out as well. Their eyes met for a while, but they quickly turned back to the phone, faces flushed, before screaming in horror yet again.

Lara tossed the device to Jun. "I can't do this," she said exasperatedly, "help me look through the photos until you find something useful!"

Jun let out a reluctant groan, but accepted the phone anyway. As he scrolled through the photos, his grimace deepened. "Argh... God, what is wrong with him... Argh, gross... Ew, what the heck... What is this... Why would he have this on here... T- There's so many women... He's such a pervert, honestly..."

"Is there... is there even anything worthwhile on there? I'm sorry, Jun, we can stop looking through it." Lara lowered her gaze. "I don't think he's the type that will leave me messages anyway."

"It's... it's okay," the dark-haired boy mumbled, "I'll... I'll keep looking for you."

Lara slumped on the bed again. Why would Ryan leave her a phone filled with these... these corrupted photos? How was he still able to irritate her even without being here?

She buried her head into her pillow again; the wet fabric felt icy cold against her cheeks. How she wished that the man was here, so she could yell at him about how much she hated him, so she could see his usual smirk and hear his usual laughter and snarky remark, so she could feel him patting her on the head and going, "My God, you're such a stupid crybaby."

Why the hell would you just leave me alone like that?

"Oh..." Jun's voice snapped Lara back from her thoughts.

"What is it?"

Jun's expression was inscrutable, but his hands were quivering. "I... I don't..."

"What is it?" Lara repeated, promptly sitting up. "Did you find something?"

"I think so..." Jun muttered, as though he was not sure if he should be showing Lara what he found. "I think it's from a really long time ago..."

Lara snatched the phone and glared at the screen. Her eyes widened, and then glazed over, as if a murky-brown fog had enwrapped her irises and clouded her vision. Once again, her grip on the phone loosened, but this time, it slipped out of her hand and crashed onto the ground.

"L- Lara?"

Slowly, she stood up, her fists clenched and her legs shivering. Her expression remained blank and eerily calm, however. She began to walk forward, ignoring the pleading stares from Jun.

"Lara..." The boy's voice had turned into a meek whisper. "M- Maybe we should talk to someone about this..."

He trailed off as the air around them started to whir. The chairs in the living room toppled over, with the adjacent cupboards crashing right on top of them. The blanket and the pillows had abandoned the bed and circled them, while the cup of smoothie spun on its axis, the liquids sloshing around violently.

"Lara, c- calm down. Let's... let's tell Arthur and figure this out together..." Jun stood up and tried to approach Lara, but the air currents were working against him.

But the young brunette was not listening anymore. In fact, there was nothing that she could see nor hear anymore; her world had been completely enshrouded with the dark fog, and was now a desolate, barren void. There was nothing there except for rage —pure, blind, unadulterated rage.

"Lara!!!" Jun shouted at the top of his lungs, but his voice faded into the loud roaring winds; it disappeared forever, along with the cries from outside the building, never reaching Lara, never reaching the source of the destruction.

"Why would he hide this from me..." Lara droned to herself. "Why is everyone hiding everything from me..."

As she continued her march forward, she had no idea how the walls of her room crumbled into pieces, how Jun was swept out of the window, how the hotel, the buildings next to the hotel, and the buildings next to those buildings, all collapsed and shattered under the force of the winds.

She did not notice any of the carnage around her, but what she did know was that: her life was a lie. Everything she had known, everything she had worked for, everyone she had trusted, they were all lies, all a bunch of liars. Something inside her grew, something she could not explain, a feeling she had never experienced before. It was like a flower inside her heart —dormant, hidden, its petals tucked in— was finally opening, revealing its blazing red core.

The world turned dark.

When Lara's vision cleared, she found herself inside a dimly-lit bedroom. Floor-to-ceiling windows lined two corners of the spacious room; the ceiling lights were turned off, so the area was illuminated only by the dazzling moonlight and the faraway city lights. In the middle of a cushioned wall laid a queen-sized bed. A woman was sitting up on the bed, blending into the shadows. Her auburn hair sprawled over the silky, maroon bedsheet, like trails of fresh blood dripping down a backdrop of old, rusty blood.

She was back on Earth. Back to the realm she grew up in, back to Elena's headquarters, and back to the room she was very familiar with: Arianna's quarters.

"Lara!" Arianna gasped. "How did you..."

Despite her visible exhaustion, Arianna quickly pulled off her blanket and shuffled to the side of the bed. The moment she saw the way the air moved around her, however, she froze.

"Lara, calm down," she warned, "you don't know how to control your Gift yet. This is a very powerful Gift, you need to start small or you'll-"

"You killed my parents."

The redhead looked as though she was struck by lightning. "W-What?" she stammered, her pale face losing even more color as Lara strolled towards her. "I- I didn't... L- Lara, I was ordered... I-"

"You betrayed them." Lara's voice was unfamiliarly calm and deep.

Arianna was trembling uncontrollably. Her hands grasped backwards as she tried to move away from the advancing brunette. "Lara, please..."

Lara, on the other hand, had never felt more serene in her life. Step by step, she neared her friend, her mentor, her confidante.

"Lara," Arianna sobbed, "please forgive me, I- I didn't mean to do it. I just wanted a Gift, I only wanted a Gift, I didn't know this was the price, I really didn't think it was going to turn out like this..." Her voice turned into frantic shriek when she realized that Lara was still coming towards her, steadfast and unwavering. "Lara, please, I took care of you, remember? I raised you up, I was nice to you! You said I'm like your mother, right? You loved me, right? L- Lara, you won't kill me, r-"

And that was all Arianna managed to say before Lara grabbed her neck. The older woman coughed and spluttered, tears streaming down her face as she pulled desperately at Lara's hands, but the younger girl's grip was firm and unmoving.

Lara stared blankly at her struggling aunt. Her lifeless eyes were unblinking as she watched the naked throat snap in half with a loud crunch. Blood splattered all over her face, and Arianna's body crumpled onto the ground like a broken doll.

Just then, the door slammed open and armed guards poured into the room. Lara did not bother facing them; she barely even noticed them firing their weapons at her. The winds hummed and buzzed around her, slapping the bullets away and smashing the windows into smithereens. Stray bullets created holes all over the room. One by one, every single guard fell onto the ground, dead from their own bullets.

Finally, Lara turned away from the fallen Arianna. What used to be a lovely, cozy bedroom was now a bloody, battered wreck.

She stepped out of the room and walked down the familiar hallway. This was the building she grew up in. It was the only place she ever knew, and she basically memorized every nook and cranny. The training rooms, the cafeteria, the trainees' quarters; this was her childhood, her entire life. She had wasted so much of her life training, studying, working towards her stupid goal. All a bunch of lies.

As she drowned in her thoughts, she did not realize that every guard, every Operative, every trainee, everybody she used to be friends with, was charging at her. But it did not matter how equipped they were; no weapons could touch Lara, no Gifts could defeat hers, and no defenses could save them from Lara's unknowing wrath. Soon, everyone, even those who chose to run away, found themselves thrown mercilessly against the walls. The cracks of their bones added to the deafening echoes of destruction, while their blood painted the white, glossy walls completely red.

The hurricane whirred stronger and faster, until the metallic walls cranked under the pressure. The building came crumbling down, falling all around the blood-drenched Lara like chalky, grey waterfalls. The teenage girl stood, silent and unfeeling, as she stared at the only place she had ever known turning into unrecognizable rocks and dusts.

"What do you think you're doing?"

Lara slowly turned around.

The First Lady was standing behind her, donning her signature tiara and long gown. Her platinum blonde hair seemed to glow; her temperate beauty and elegant calmness was a stark contrast against the dull, ashen surroundings. It was as if she was an angel sent down from heaven, tasked to save the world from an imminent threat.

"Elena," Lara said.

"Lara," Elena answered coolly. She was the only person not affected by the growing windstorm around her. "What happened to Ryan? Did he die?"

Ryan.

Lara's eyes twitched. A wave of emotions hit her, instantly jolting her out of her trance state.

Ryan.

"Did you kill him to get his Gift?" Elena asked with a derisive smirk. "I didn't know you were the cruel type, Lara."

"You." Lara's voice was shrill and shaky. "You are the one responsible for everything."

"No, you are." Elena lifted her hands. "Have you looked around, my child? This is all you. You're the real terror here."

Lara blinked. For the first time, the fog cleared from her brain and she finally took in the surroundings. Immediately, the images of the bloodied corpses and debris flooded her vision. She gasped, and staggered a little; the winds came to a complete halt.

"No, no, no..." she mumbled. "What have I done..."

Elena smiled. She raised a pistol.

"Just die already."

The words were spoken with so much force that Lara felt them weigh down all over her body. They reverberated throughout her head; her skull throbbed in pain and her heart clenched up.

Then, Elena pressed the trigger, and time seemed to slow down. Lara watched helplessly as the bullet flew towards her. She wanted to move, to dodge, to run away, but an invisible force was holding her back from it.

The bullet touched her forehead, and she exploded.

Lara screamed. All the pain, confusion, sadness, grief, anger; every emotion that was brewing inside her, was let out into one harrowing, ear-piercing scream. A strong blast of wind ejected from her, blasting everything away; its force was unmatched by any atomic bombs, any massive air strikes, any weapons of mass destruction known to mankind. Everything was annihilated at once; everything, including what was left of the building; everything, including the shell-shocked First Lady; everything, including the rest of the city, country... Earth.

In the aftermath, everything had become nothing. As far as Lara could see, there was nothing. All through the horizon, it was plain, empty, nothing.

Lara whimpered and fell onto her knees.

The sky rumbled. Rain plunged from the dark clouds as tears flowed from Lara's eyes. The grayness of the heavens seemed to be embracing the grayness of the ruins, like a mother caressing her newborn baby.

Earth was reborn.

And the sole survivor, the last of the First Gift, sat alone and forsaken, doused in the torrent of rains.

***

Epilogue

----

six years ago —

"Welcome to Nightlaza".

These holographic words floated above the square entrance of the bar, casting a soft blue glow all over the room. The metallic shine of the tables added to the elegant ambience, while the mocha brick walls gave the place a cozier feeling. A handful of people sat on the leather couches, chatting and sipping on drinks. Occasionally, they would place their finished drinks on the round coffee table; a hole would open up to swallow the empty glass, and a new glass of drink would take its place.

Across the entrance stood a giant shelf filled with liquor bottles, each of them glistening with a similar blue color. Behind the bar table was Darren, the only bartender available for the day. His silky blond hair was pulled into a neat bun, and he was wiping on a wine glass idly —a meaningless activity as all cups and glasses were automatically rinsed and cleaned, but there was really nothing else to do on a lazy Tuesday evening.

A faint bell ring notified him of a new customer, and he peeled his eyes away from the over-cleaned wine glass. Sauntering towards the bar table was a tall, brown-haired man. He was wearing a navy blue shirt that was way too tight for him. His permanent smirk and unfairly long eyelashes made Darren's hands itch to curl up into fists.

Oh, Darren definitely recognized this guy. He was one of them. An Operative.

Great, just great. Darren rolled his eyes and turned his attention back to his mundane task. This was why he hated working in this place. Being a reasonable distance from the First Lady's headquarters, the Nightlaza bar was quite a hot spot for Operatives to visit. They frequented the bar in large groups and acted like a gang of thugs, making a huge ruckus and turning this laidback bar into a rowdy strip club within minutes.

As he was silently reminding himself to hunt for a new job, the newcomer settled right in front of him. "Hey, can I get a beer?"

Darren did not even bother looking up at him. "ID, please."

"ID?" the Operative scoffed. "Caroline never checks for ID."

Of course she didn't. To his boss, anyone old enough to become an Operative was old enough to drink. Not to him, though. He's not serving any underaged Operative. Or any Operative, for that matter.

"I'm not Caroline," Darren said flatly. "ID, please."

"Oh, come on, dude. I'm turning twenty-one real soon, like, in a few months, I swear."

Darren did not budge as he continued obsessing over the wine glass.

"Geez, who do I need to kill to get a beer around here?" the Operative complained as he threw his hands up in an exaggerated manner.

A small smile crept across Darren's face. "Do you mean that? You'd kill for a beer?"

The brunet perked up at the question. "Yes, sir. I'd literally kill for a good beer right now."

"Okay, then." Darren stared right into the man's twinkling, brown eyes. "I can give you a beer for free if you can kill someone for me."

"Oh?" The Operative raised his eyebrows. "Interesting. You've come to the right person, you know. I'm very skilled at killing people, whether I like it or not. Who is it?"

"You."

There was a long, awkward pause after that, while the two men locked eyes with each other uncomfortably. Darren suddenly regretted his poorly thought out joke. Operatives were insane creatures that were given those witch-like magic called Gifts. What if this man could blast his head off with a fireball, or something? Maybe he shouldn't have tried to provoke someone like that...

To his surprise, the brunet chortled. "Sure, I'll do it," he said with a wide grin. "Come on, give me a pint of your best, most expensive, draft beer."

Darren did not expect a reply like that, and so he was rendered speechless. Reluctantly, he gave the Operative a full mug of beer.

"Finally, thank you," the Operative said before immediately chugging down half the cup. He wiped his mouth and let out a relieved sigh. "So, not-Caroline, what do people usually call you?"

"Darren..."

"Darren. Cute name," he said with a wink. "I'm Ryan. Nice to meet you."

Darren frowned in response, and went back to cleaning more cups and glasses. He did not want to get too friendly with an Operative, especially someone who was as obnoxious as this guy. But it turned out that it was impossible ignoring someone who was not only sitting right in front of him, but also staring at him as if he was the most interesting artwork at a museum.

"Stop looking at me like that," Darren grumbled.

That did not seem to deter Ryan at all. "Why not?"

"Where are your friends? Don't you Operatives usually come here in packs like horny werewolves? You a loner, or something?"

Ryan shrugged. "It's a Tuesday. Nobody wants to come along. They're all training."

"And you don't need to train?"

"Oh, I need to. I'm actually the one Operative that needs to train the most. I just don't feel like it." With a large swig, he finished his beer. "Can I get another round?" Then, he laughed at Darren's irked glare. "Hey, I'm giving my life up for this, and I can't even get unlimited rounds of beer?"

Darren groaned as he prepared another mug of beer for the insatiable customer. "Are you trying to die by alcohol overdose?"

"Perhaps." Ryan chuckled.

Afterwards, the Operative kept initiating conversations, although it would always be cut short by Darren, who was adamant in keeping all their interactions as minimal as possible.

As the night progressed, however, Darren could not help but notice Ryan's gradual descent into sorrow. It was like the man had a wall erected around his heart, and the more he drank, the more the wall crumbled. That mischievous, lighthearted twinkle faded away, while a dull glaze of agony took over. Darren had seen enough people come and go during his bartending days to know that this guy had... issues. Major issues.

One more reason not to get involved with him.

Ryan managed to finish a few more pints before slumping onto the bar table, absolutely wasted, and mumbling to himself like a madman. Darren watched in exasperation, periodically reaching out to stop the drunken man from falling to the ground whenever he rolled over in slumber.

At last, it was 2 a.m. His shift had come to an end, but Ryan was still here.

Darren sighed and poked at the bed of curly, brown hair. "Hey, are you dead?"

Ryan stirred, but remained unconscious.

"Seriously, why do people drink so much if they're not able to take it?"

Staring at the Operative, Darren mused for a while. He could either leave this guy in the bar overnight, or bring him to his place for now.

Letting out yet another sigh, he reluctantly decided on the latter. He was definitely charging him extra for this.

It turned out that the tall man was a lot heavier than he looked, and it was not an easy feat to heave him out of the bar. When they finally made it to his small studio apartment, Darren was sure he had exercised enough for the rest of the year.

Exhausted, he dropped Ryan onto his own bed, which he immediately realized to be a terrible idea. Why did he do that? Where was he, the person who actually paid the rent, going to sleep? He groaned out loud when he saw Ryan roll over and spread himself out, as though he owned the entire bed. Great, now he definitely did not have any space for himself.

As he leaned over to push Ryan to one side, he heard him mumble again. But for the first time all night, it was something that was coherent.

"Lara... I'm sorry..."

Lara?

Darren felt like he was punched in the gut. So this guy had a girlfriend this whole time? Why the hell was he looking at him like that the whole night then? His jaw clenched in ire. He should have known that these Operatives should never be trusted. Instantly, all semblance of niceness and prudence flew out the window as Darren forcefully yanked Ryan up by the collar and the hair.

"Ow, ow, ow!" Ryan yelped, as he subconsciously pushed his hands out in protest.

"You! Are! Sleeping! On the! Couch! Get! Off!" Darren snapped, slapping Ryan's hands away after every sentence.

Suddenly, Ryan lunged at him. They both crashed onto the bed, with Ryan's arms wrapped around Darren's waist.

"Hey, if you're awake, go home!" Darren exclaimed, struggling under the Operative's weight. His hair tie had come off during the scuffle, causing his long, blond hair to sprawl messily around his torso. As if by instinct, Ryan buried his head into Darren's hair, his arms still tightly holding onto Darren.

"Argh, get off me!" Darren squirmed around, but Ryan was a lot stronger than him. "Go back to your girlfriend, you idiot!"

"Mom..." Ryan croaked.

Hearing that, Darren stopped moving. The brunet took the chance and pushed his head further into the cloak of blond hair. His head landed onto Darren's shoulder, while his warm breath, still stinking of alcohol, sent a strangely comforting sensation down Darren's neck.

Darren let out a long, resigned sign. Hesitantly, he placed a hand on Ryan's head. The sleeping Ryan did not look as annoying and punchable as before, which was a nice change. Then, with a pounding heart, Darren closed his eyes and tried to sleep.

The next morning, Darren woke up alone. A plate of freshly cooked eggs and bacon sat on his bedside table, but Ryan was nowhere to be seen.

— —

Ryan finally showed up to the bar more than a week later. Not that Darren had been waiting for him or anything. And this time, he had come with his Operative friends. They hung around in a corner of the bar with a group of ladies for most of the night. Not that Darren was upset about that or anything.

After a while, Ryan left the group and approached the bar table. "Hey there," he said with his usual aggravating smirk. "Nice seeing you again."

Darren pursed his lips and averted his face. "Why are you still alive?" he spat. "When are you going to pay up for your beer?"

Ryan looked mildly taken aback before he doubled over in laughter. "Sorry, sorry. I promise you, I'll pay you back one day, okay?"

"Shut the fuck up..." The Operative's nonchalant attitude made Darren even more sullen. "So who's Lara? Your girlfriend?"

"What? Are you jealous?" Ryan raised his eyebrows. "You spent a night with me and you're already so attached? I mean, understandable, I know I have that effect on people."

Darren rolled his eyes. "You're literally the worst person I've ever met."

"You're probably right." Ryan chuckled. Then, his smile subsided when he added, "Lara's my sister, by the way."

"Oh." Darren's expression softened. "Is your sister an Operative too?" he whispered.

Ryan shook his head. "Not yet."

"Not yet?"

"Madam is setting her up to be one." Ryan lowered his head. "And she really wants to be one too."

Darren stared at the unusually solemn Operative. They sat in silence for a while, before he muttered under his breath, "Why would anybody want to become an Operative?"

Ryan shrugged. "She thinks it's cool. Like superheroes, fighting for justice, ending the reigns of terror of the Turned Realms, blah blah blah. I keep trying to tell her that it's a bad idea but she's not getting it. She really looks up to Operatives." He paused for a while before adding, "Not me, though. She thinks I'm a loser."

Darren snorted. "Damn straight you are."

The signature smirk came back onto Ryan's face. "Says the college dropout working in the shittiest bar in town."

"How do you-" Darren's ears turned pink. "I- I couldn't afford it anymore, okay."

Ryan laughed as he reached his hand out to squeeze Darren's cheek. "Who cares about college anyway. Get out of here. Save up your money and go to a different realm."

Darren slapped the Operative's hand away, scowling. "I don't want to. I'm from here. My family was from here. I'm never leaving Earth."

"That's the stupidest reason I've ever heard," Ryan said with a snort. "If you were to say something about how the other realms might discriminate against Earthlings or how your life might be slightly harder because of that, I might understand. But you were born here? That's bull." He glanced at Darren. "Your family isn't even here anymore too, why do you care?"

Darren felt his blood boil. Did this guy... sneak around his apartment the other day? He had never wanted to stick his fist into someone's eye more badly in his entire life. With a pair of trembling hands, he pulled Ryan out of his seat by the collar. "Suck a dick, asshole."

"Sure, yeah." The brunet wiggled his eyebrows cheekily. "I can do that for you."

This time, Darren's entire head turned pink. He quickly pushed Ryan away. "S- Shut the fuck up..."

Ryan tried to laugh, but his face contorted into a wince as his hand shot up to his chest. Darren was startled by that reaction, and he suddenly noticed that there was a new scar on Ryan's neck.

"What's wrong with you?" Darren asked. He tried to touch the scar but Ryan jerked away.

"Nothing," he said curtly. When he noticed Caroline walking towards them, his tone changed again. "Although be more careful next time, Darren, I can't stay over too late. Us Operatives have curfews, you know?"

That annoying bastard had said it loud enough for Darren's boss to hear, which prompted an astonished gasp from her. "Oh. My. God. Are the two of you together?" Caroline gushed, clasping her hands together. "Darren! Why didn't you tell me?"

"No, no!" Darren shook his hands around, flustered. "Caroline, it's not what you th-"

Caroline squealed and dashed off anyway, presumably to tell everyone in the bar and everyone in the area about this news.

Darren groaned and buried his head into hands. "You just killed my chance of ever getting into a real relationship."

"Hey, don't blame your virginity on me, it's not my fault."

"I can't believe an underaged person is saying this shit to me."

Once again, Ryan laughed. Curiously, his smile no longer felt aggravating; it was actually pleasant and amicable. So he was perfectly capable of being a normal, nice person; why was he always coating everything he did with a feigned layer of arrogance, then? It was as if he was acting the role of a wretched jerk all the time, as if he was trying his best to stop people from liking him, from knowing who he really was.

Something grew inside Darren's heart, something that made his stomach flutter and his chest tickle. It was like a tiny orchid within him —petals as white as Ryan's skin— was slowly opening up to this dark, bleak world.

He gave Ryan a gentle smack on the head, before taking his now-empty mug for a refill.

— present —

Darren leaned on his hand as he took a sip of his whiskey. The famous Nightlaza bar was completely empty. The holographic welcome message was still shimmering above the entrance, while the glossy tables had unfinished glasses and cups sprawled all over them.

He had sent out a warning notice for people to get out of Earth last night; he wasn't sure if everyone complied, but it seemed that at least his colleagues and the customers who frequented the bar listened to him.

But he wasn't leaving, though. Earth was his home, and his family's home. Nobody can make him leave. Not even Ryan.

He glanced at the message that was still hovering above his phone screen.

"hey dude, im finally paying you back for that beer six years agosorry for being so late lolbut if you can see my face right now, i assure u im paying back with interest lmaoanyway, shit is for real now, i suggest u leave earth asap please, leave

please

anyway, wont see u for a while, so go find someone actually deserving of you to hook up withdont miss me too much, fag"

The grip around the whiskey glass tightened, and then Darren chugged the rest of the liquid down.

Asshole. The stupid message was all that Ryan had left for him. Did the past six years mean nothing to him? Or had Darren been in a one-sided relationship this whole time?

Come to think of it, even after six years, he still didn't really know much about Ryan. That selfish guy had kept everything to himself, putting on a front at all times. Occasionally, he would reveal a tiny glimpse of his true self, but it would be immediately shut down again. Why was he like this? Why did he insist on being an obnoxious asshole, even to his death?

Darren poured himself another cup of whiskey as he scrolled through his phone. He scrolled through the images of his parents, back when he had just been a toddler; his sister, right before her brain surgery, looking so hopeful, so optimistic, so cheerful; and lastly, Ryan's sleeping face. The Operative had hated having his photo taken, and so Darren only had these poorly-taken sneak shots to look back on.

His eyes lingered on the photo. Ryan's small, upturned nose was pressing against the pillow, while the dim moonlight painted a few streaks of yellow across his high cheekbones. It was almost unfair just how gorgeous he looked. Darren took a few more swigs before looking out the window.

In the horizons, there was a windstorm. It swirled, shaking the ground, conjoining the gray sky with the earth. Darren watched it grow in size, first slowly, and then at a speed he could never imagine. A wave of ashen clouds flew towards the bar, swallowing everything it touched into itself.

His hands quivered. This was the most terrifying thing Darren had ever seen in his life. Whoever responsible for this must be one hell of a monster. He closed his eyes and, for the last time, drank his whiskey.

I'll see you in hell, asshole. And then I'll slap your face for this.

***